DAVID WEAVER PRESENTS

a Thug's LOVE 3

JESSICA N. WATKINS

PREVIOUSLY ON A THUG'S LOVE

KING

I sat waiting at the crib for hours. I was just sitting in the living room with the lights off, not knowing what to do. I couldn't eat, sleep or drink. I just sat there praying that Kennedy would show up while I stalked everyone, even her father, hoping that she and Kayla were with one of them. But each time, everyone swore that they hadn't heard from her. And as the sun went down and the living room grew dark, I knew that if she was coming home, she would have by now.

Enraged by my own stupidity, I left, ready to kick down doors to find her and my daughter. I knew she wouldn't be at Meech's house, so I went to Dolla and Jada's first.

"I'm serious! She's not here!" Jada screeched, as I gently pushed by her.

I searched every room and closet on the first floor as she called after me.

"King! What's wrong? Calm down!" she shouted, as she followed me up the stairs.

Again, I searched every room and closet. I even searched the kids' rooms. They looked at me like I was crazy as I searched every inch of the space, even under the beds.

"King!" Jada shouted another warning at me as I stormed down the stairs. Again, she was on my heels. "What the fuck is going on? Should I be worried?"

"She's upset," I finally answered. "She overheard something fucked up, and I guess she left. She must have forgotten her phone. I can't..." I took a deep breath, still unable to catch it. My fucking head was spinning. "I can't find her, Jada."

"What did she overhear?" Her arms were folded as she glared at me, and I froze. I couldn't even allow the words to leave my throat.

"I gotta go," I said, as I went to her front door and flung it open. "Call me if you hear from her, please."

And then I ran to my car without even waiting for her reply.

DOLLA

"He did what?" I asked Jada, as I got up to leave the office of the convenience store.

"He came in here, busting open doors, closets and all kinds of shit!" Jada squealed. "The nigga is spazzing! He can't find Kennedy anywhere."

"You haven't heard from her for real?" I asked.

"No. And she don't have her phone. She knows my number by heart, though, so I hope she'll call me."

"A'ight, bae," I told her as I put about a hundred thousand dollars in twenties, fives, and ones inside of the wall safe. "I'll call that nigga to see what's going on. I'll be home in a minute. I'm leaving now."

"Okay."

I hung up, leaving the office and pushing the necessary numbers to call King when the phone started to ring.

It was Meagan.

"What's up?" I answered, hoping that she hadn't sat on my truth all day and was now stirring in anger.

Yet, instead of anger, I heard tears. "H-Hello? Brandon?"

It wasn't Meagan's voice that I heard. It was her mother's. I stopped dead in my tracks in the middle of the convenience store. The cashier looked at me oddly as I stared blankly, wondering why Meagan's mother would be calling me in tears.

"It's me, Miss Rachel," I told her. "What's wrong?"

"There's…" Her tears made her unable to speak. "T-there's been an…an accident. I need you to come t-to the hospital." Then she broke down in uncontrollable sobs.

I raced out of the store and toward my car.

"Miss Rachel." I was trying to get her attention while I jumped into the car and started it. "Miss Rachel, what happened? What's wrong? Are the babies okay?"

"Yes, they're okay. But…it's Meagan. It's bad. Just come right away. We're at the University of Chicago. Hurry!"

****

Meagan had been in a horrific car accident an hour before her mother called me. She was texting and driving on the expressway and rear-ended a semi at seventy miles per hour. Her body was mangled, and she had undergone emergency surgery. There was nothing that the doctors could tell us. As we sat in the waiting room, awaiting some news from the surgeons, we didn't even know if she would survive or not.

At nearly midnight, Meagan was still in surgery. The twins became fussy. Luckily, they had been with their grandmother at the time of the accident.

"Why don't you take them home?"

Not even realizing it, I looked at her like she had lost her damn mind. And that's when I realized that this woman probably didn't even know my situation.

"I can stay here and help you watch them," I insisted.

"They need to go home. They're hungry. I've run out of diapers and milk, and honestly, hearing them cry is just making this worse. I can't tend to them *and* worry about Meagan..." Then her eyes watered up. "This is just too much... They don't need to be in this hospital with these germs anyway."

I sat there stuck, and she looked at me, wondering what the fuck my hesitation was about. Then she started to put their things into the diaper bag. I was still in a daze as she put Brandon, who she was holding, into his car seat.

I didn't want to argue with this woman. She was going through enough. Doctors were trying to save her daughter's life. She was even crying as she took Bianca from me and strapped her into her car seat too.

"Do you need help taking them to the car?" she asked as she wiped tears away. But there was no use. She would wipe some tears away, and more would just take their place.

I slowly shook my head and left as the woman asked me to.

"I'll call you when I have some news," I heard her say.

"Okay," weakly left my mouth as I carried the twins out.

I walked down the hall, wondering what the fuck to do! I thought maybe I could just take them to Meagan's house because going home was *not* an option. But shit, staying out all night wasn't an option either. Jada had already been texting the hell out of me, wondering where the hell I was, as I'd sat in the hospital for hours.

As I walked through the parking lot, I wracked my brain, trying to come up with a plan. I even thought about taking the twins to one of the girls instead, but last I'd heard, Kennedy was still missing. I quickly remembered that Siren was a psychopath that I wasn't desperate enough to allow to help me. As I strapped them into the backseat, I even considered taking them to King or Meech, but they weren't answering their phones.

As I got into the driver's seat, Brandon started to cry, and in response, Bianca did too.

"Fuck!" I shouted at the top of my lungs as I punched the steering wheel. I was angry as I realized that I had no other options.

There wasn't anything that I could do. I had to take them home.

As I reluctantly pulled out of the parking lot, I turned on the radio to drown out my thoughts.

♪ I'm rushing home
She said she's packing her things
And she's leaving the keys to
the front door
Should I have known,
That it would happen once again
Was it something I could've
done to make her stay ♪

One Chance's lyrics drowned out the twins' cries but only magnified how fucked up this shit was going to be. Jada had been the true, textbook example of a ride or die chick. I had fucked up so much in the past that I could only pray that Jada would find some forgiveness in her heart.

For twenty minutes, I prayed for a miracle—for God to make a way for me to get out of walking into my house with these kids. When my cell phone rang, displaying Miss Rachel's number, I thought He'd answered my prayers.

"Hel-"

But that was far from the case. My prayers had most definitely gone unanswered.

"Oh God!"

My heart beat with reluctance as I heard the sheer terror and hurt in Miss Rachel's cries. "She's gone! She's gone, Brandon! She didn't make it! Oh my God...!"

I cringed as it all became too real. Miss Rachel was crying so desperately that I wanted to turn the car around and go back to console her.

Tears pooled in my eyes as I told her, "I'm coming back." I wasn't trying to avoid taking the kids home. I really wanted to be there for Miss Rachel, and I felt like I should be there. Meagan was never my woman, and I didn't love her, but I liked her a lot. She was a good person, and I would truly miss her laugh. She had such a bright future ahead of her. She didn't deserve to die so soon.

Then I thought of my kids, who would never know her, and my heart broke.

"No," Miss Rachel insisted, through tears. "I don't want them here. Meagan's father's flight landed a little while ago. He should be here soon, so I won't be alone." Her cries took over her words. She was breaking down yet again. "Jesus! I can't believe she's gone! My babyyyy!" I stayed quiet, listening to her as a tear fell down my cheek. After a few minutes, she was able to control her tears enough to say, "Just take care of my grandbabies, Brandon. I have to go."

Just as she hung up, I realized that I was approaching my block. I sighed heavily, attempting to gather my composure as I noticed the silence. The babies were asleep. As I turned into my driveway, there were no words for how heavy and empty I felt. Meagan was dead, and now I was about to emotionally kill Jada the moment that I walked through the door with these babies. This shit was causing me pain that a nigga like me had never felt before. I had never been so emotionally torn, and I didn't know what to do or how to fix it. What I did know was that I couldn't sit in the car forever.

I took a deep breath and killed the engine. "C'mon y'all," I said quietly, to the sleeping twins. "Let's go break my baby's heart."

KING

After leaving Jada's crib, I went to Kennedy's parents' home, doing the same thing—telling them respectfully that I was searching every inch of their house whether they liked it or not, but I never found her. I knew that she was somewhere hiding from me, but I had checked all of her resources, so where could she be? Shit, as I sat in the car outside of her father's home, I even called every major hotel asking if a Kennedy Carter had checked in; but after the tenth hotel, I got nowhere, and I was starting feel like a mad man.

I sat in my car at a gas station near her father's house, not knowing where to go next. I hoped that maybe she had gone back home by now, so I started the car and prepared to go home when I felt a constant vibration in my pocket.

My phone was in my hand, so I wondered for a second, and then realized that I had shoved Kennedy's phone into my pocket. I frantically reached into my pocket, hoping that she was calling.

It wasn't her calling, however. The vibration was just notifications. I had her password because I'd set the phone up for her when I bought it. I hoped that she hadn't changed it yet. She hadn't, so I was able to see the missed calls that had come since I had it. Her mother, father, and Jada had blown her phone up, and the last call was Jada again. However, there was a number that hadn't been stored in the phone that had called quite a few times earlier that day and then stopped. When I looked at the time, I realized that it had come in right around the time she would have normally come home and overheard me and Meech. Then I noticed words flashing at the top of the screen, notifying text messages. I scrolled to the inbox and saw that the same unsaved number had texted her around the time of the call.

773-413-0999: *What's up? It's Dre, baby. Answer the phone. I'm out. Come see me. 8343 S. Wolcott.*

"The fuck?" I muttered. Instantly, I got heated!

Dre? Baby? Who the fuck is this nigga?

The text hadn't been opened, but she could have read that shit in the notifications on the top of the screen. Although Kennedy and I had only been together for two years before she went to prison, for five years we had been spiritually and emotionally connected. Our bond was tighter than a couple that had been married for thirty years, and I thought our loyalty was stronger than this. But shit, it seemed that I hadn't been the only one hiding something!

Talk about a nigga being pissed? I was heated! I couldn't get to that address fast enough! A nigga was steaming as I bent corners and blocks at damn near a hundred miles an hour. Once I arrived at the address and pulled in front of the small, single-family home, I reached into the glove compartment and got my burner.

Whoever this nigga was, he was about to get *kilt*, and then I was going to drag Kennedy's ass out of there with Kayla on my hip.

I climbed out of the car, slammed the door shut, and raced toward the house. I banged on the door with the butt of my gun and even attempted to kick that motherfucker down! Within seconds, some lil' nigga with green-ass eyes swung the door open, trying to look all threatening and shit, but was met with a gun in his face, so quickly he bitched up.

"Aye, man! What the fuck?!" he shouted with his hands up.

I forced my way inside, not even closing the door behind me. "Where the fuck is she?"

"Who?" He stared at me, wondering who the fuck was I was talking about.

My eyes burned into his as my nose flared. I grabbed his little ass around the neck while I pointed the gun straight at his temple. "Don't fucking play with me!"

Then it was like something dawned on him. As he stared at me, it was like something hit him and he realized something. "King?" he asked.

"Yeah, nigga, King! Now where the fuck is Kennedy?"

He had the nerve to fucking chuckle like shit was sweet, and there wasn't a gun to his head. I squeezed his neck tighter, and he threw his hands further into the air in surrender. "Aye! Aye!

Cool out. It ain't like that. I'm Dre...*Drea*...her cellmate from the pen, man."

Drea. Kennedy had told me about her and Ms. Jerry many times.

I let her neck go and put the gun down.

"She didn't know I was getting out this morning. I wanted to surprise her, but she hasn't hit me back." She noticed my frustration and asked, "You don't know where she's at?"

"Nah. I'm looking for her. She left her phone. I thought she might be here. Mind if I look around?"

"You don't believe me?" she asked, chuckling.

I gave her a cold, emotionless stare, giving her my answer.

"Go ahead," she nodded. "But this is my mama's house, so respect her shit."

She stayed in the living room while I looked through the small, two bedroom home. There was no sign of Kennedy or Kayla anywhere.

When I walked back into the living room, Dre was sitting comfortably on the couch. She seemed to notice that my demeanor had changed. I had gone from deadly to somber. This had been my last hope. Now I just felt hopeless.

"What's wrong? She's missing or something?" Dre asked.

"Kinda. She's mad at me, so hasn't come home yet." Then I just walked by Dre and went straight for the door. "If you talk to Ms. Jerry, ask her if she's talked to Kennedy."

I heard Dre sigh heavily. "I'm not gon' talk to Ms. Jerry. She's dead. She died Wednesday night."

Fuck. My steps halted slightly, and I shook my head. *Something else that's going to break her heart.*

"Please tell her to call me when you find her," Dre said, as I walked out of the door.

I kept walking toward my ride. My feet were barely able to move because my body was so weighed down with guilt. I couldn't believe that I was putting Kennedy through this and that I couldn't hold her to make it better. For three years, I hadn't been able to hold her to make it feel better, and now I was right back in the same situation because of some shit I had done. As I rode to the crib, I anticipated an angry Kennedy being there.

As I pulled into the garage, regret filled my heart when I realized that her car was nowhere to be found. I walked into a pitch black house, and my heart sank. She wasn't there, and by the looks of it, she hadn't been there.

I collapsed on the couch, feeling lost and helpless. I had forgotten about everything else, including Elijah and Siren. All I wanted was Kennedy. I had spent years feeling an unbearable yearning for that woman, and here that intolerable feeling was again. I hated it. I just wanted her to come back so that the feeling would go away.

I lay there until the sun came up, and my body began to heave as I realized that I had possibly lost Kennedy forever.

"Urrrgh!" I was sick to my fucking stomach as I began to dry heave. "Fuck!"

I rolled off of the couch and onto my knees. My head slowly fell to the carpet as my fingers clutched the fibers of it in anguish. I was a hurting man. I had spent three years missing Kennedy, and I had never wanted to feel that heartbreak again. Yet I was, just three weeks later. My body was rejecting that fucked up feeling, attempting to force it out through my throat.

Tears filled my eyes as they squeezed tightly together and my mind screamed, *Where the fuck is she?*

CHAPTER ONE

JADA

Dolla had me completely and utterly fucked up. If this was the first time that he'd let my calls go unanswered for this long, I wouldn't give a fuck. Hell, if it was the second or third time, I wouldn't be trippin' like *this*. But it wasn't the first, second, third, or, hell, even the fifteenth time. It was the *umpteenth* motherfuckin' time that I had called this nigga since I was sixteen years old, and he had blatantly ignored by calls as if I meant fucking nothing to him!

Unanswered calls may not mean shit for a regular nigga, but we ain't talkin' about a regular nigga. We're talkin' about a man who has told me with a straight face that he wasn't on shit, but I later found out that the motherfucker was damn near in a whole relationship with another bitch while I was on the block selling his dope like a goofy. Therefore, this had far surpassed a man just not answering his phone. This was evidence that this nigga was once again - after *allllllll* that I had done for him, after all that I had done for his crew- playing me like a motherfucking goofy!

And that was *not* okay.

I had even called both Meech and King on some nonchalant shit just to see what they were doing, and they easily told me that they weren't on shit. So, Dolla wasn't with them. I had left my kids in the house just to drive past all the spots that the crew owned and all the properties that Dolla owned to confirm that he wasn't at any of those places either. So, as this bitch ignored my calls and sent me text messages saying that he was "handling business," I knew he was lying to me! That shit *hurt*! I had just shot my best-motherfucking-friend off the strength that I was protecting, most of all, *him*! And this bitch had the nerve to play me?

Fuck that!

I had paced the living room floor so much that I had probably worn the tan colored carpet completely out. Mad was an understatement. I had surpassed being heartbroken. I felt like I was going to die, as I clutched the trigger of Dolla's pistol, tears running races down my face.

"I hate that bitch," I growled angrily.

I did. I *really* hated Dolla at this point, and I wanted him to feel the pain that I was feeling. The next day, when I sobered up, I would probably feel like a piece of shit for killing my baby's father. Yet, at that moment, the tequila, which I had drank for hours as that bitch had the nerve to continuously feed me lies through text messages while he ignored my calls, had me all too willing to show this motherfucker who he *thought* he was playing with.

Eight years. For eight long ass motherfucking years, I flipped dope with him. I hugged that block with that motherfucker in ten-degree weather in the middle of many Chicago winters. I moved dope for him while he screwed bitch after bitch, while he hit me, while he never asked me to marry him. Now, after we were finally getting shit right, this motherfucker wanted to play ... *again*.

"Stupid bitch," I spat.

I had no more fight left in me. Shit, there was no fight to be had. There was no motherfuckin' arguments or words to be said.

I was gonna kill his ass.

Plain and motherfucking simple.

In the back of my mind, I just knew that once I saw his face, I would change my mind, but as I heard those keys in the door and saw the time, the thought of him being dead was the only fucking thing that would make this horrible feeling go away.

There I was, standing in the middle of the floor with my hand clutching the trigger, watching the locks turn. I was pretty sure that I looked like a fucking mad woman, barefoot with my hair in a wild bun and nothing on but a t-shirt and panties. I had tossed and turned for hours, wondering what bitch Dolla was laying up under, while drinking the hurt away. As the door slowly opened, I couldn't believe that this bitch was just gon' show up acting as if he was just somewhere "handling business."

I was so tired of –

"The fuck?!" I shrieked in response to the sight in front of me.

You would have thought that once I saw the two babies, I would have put down the gun, but it only made me hug the trigger tighter.

Dolla jumped at the sight of a gun being pointed at his head. "What the fuck is you doin'?!" he asked, sitting the car seats down in the doorway.

I wasn't even looking at him. I was staring at those babies, who were too fresh to have any features that I tried hard to recognize.

"Who the fuck are they?!" I shouted as I pointed the gun towards one of the car seats.

Dolla looked at me like I was as psycho as I felt. He cautiously stepped in front of the car seat that I was pointing towards. "Where the kids at?" he asked.

"Don't ask me about *my* kids! Why do you have *these* babies with you?! WHO ARE THEY?"

What was so fucked up was that Dolla never asked me to put the gun down. It wasn't that he didn't think I wouldn't pull the trigger either. I had pulled a lot of triggers in my day. Shit, I just tried to kill my best friend, who I had known longer than him, so he knew I had no problem poppin' his ass. He stood in front of me, right in line with the barrel, with the saddest look on his face, like he expected and welcomed death.

"Mama, what's wrong?"

As soon as I heard my son's voice, my motherly instincts kicked in, and I turned my back to Dolla to glance towards the stairs at Brandon's concerned face. Fortunately for Dolla, my guard was down, so he took the opportunity to snatch the gun out of my hand.

My neck snapped back towards him. My plan was to use the gun to kill him, but I could have killed him with the look in my eyes.

"Who are they?" I heard Brandon's young, squeaky voice ask.

"Go back to bed, Brandon," his father ordered softly.

However, Brandon's curiosity got the best of him, causing him to further question his dad, "But who-"

"Go...back...to...bed."

The chastising baritone of his father's voice made him scurry up the stairs.

I shot eyes full of rage and fury at Dolla. "You can't make me go to bed, bitch. Whose babies are these? And why the fuck are they in my gawd damn house?"

This was when I expected to hear that one of his boys needed an emergency babysitter, that somebody's baby's mama was deathly ill or got shot, so Dolla had to take the kids... Something!

But I was not, in no way, expecting the shit that this bitch said to me!

"They mine," he mumbled as his guilty eyes fell shamefully away from mine. "These are my kids."

I lost it! I fucking lost it! I said no words. I lunged for the gun as if I could really get it out of his hands, but I was *that* fucking angry; I thought that no matter how much bigger and stronger he was than me that I could claw, scratch and bite that gun out of his hands. One of us was going to die that night- me, him, one of those gawd damn babies or both – because I was fighting to get my finger on that trigger and was ready to squeeze it no matter whose hand the gun was in and no matter what direction it was pointing in.

Somebody was going to die.

Somebody *had* to die.

That was the only way I would feel any redemption. It was the only way that this pain would be worth feeling. I was dying a slow death on the inside. I felt like I would kill myself at any moment.

Somebody had to die with me.

"Stop! Calm down!" Dolla fussed as we wrestled.

"Fuck you, bitch! I hate you! How could you do this to me?!"

I hated that I was crying. I hated that I sounded weak. But if I sounded weak, those motherfucking blows that I landed on Dolla showed his ass that I was far from a weak bitch.

As we continued to wrestle, I felt us knock over one of the car seats. The baby started to cry, and my motherly instincts kicked in, so I stopped. I hated that there was a part of me that actually gave a fuck if that little bastard was hurt. As I stood watching Dolla rush to check on the baby, I knew that that part of me that cared for that baby was the weak ass, loving, nurturing, dumb-as-shit side of me that led me to stand by this bitch no matter what he did to me for all these years.

I ran past him, up the stairs and into Brandon's room. Brandon was still up, so his eyes darted at me questionably. He knew something was wrong.

"Get up and get dressed," I ordered as I cut on the light.

Still, he looked at me, with his young eyes full of wonder. "Wh-"

"Just do what I said!" I shouted. "NOW!"

Then I stormed out and into Brittany's room. She was already stirring in her sleep. I assumed she had heard me screaming at the top of my lungs. I flipped her light on, and her eyes fought to adjust to the sudden seventy-five watts.

"Brittany, get up." I was practically dragging her out of the bed as I fought to gain some type of composure. I didn't want to cry in front of my kids, but I couldn't help it.

"What's wrong, Mama?"

"We gotta go, baby."

Though Brittany was only a year older than her brother, being a girl caused her to mature much faster. It was that and the fact that her little ass would listen to my phone calls. Her eight-year-old ass wanted to be a big girl so bad, so she recognized my tears. She knew that her daddy had done something and I was leaving, so she got dressed with no question. As soon as I darted out of the room, I saw Dolla rushing towards me with one of those babies in his arms. I guessed that the other one was still sleeping.

"Baby, let me explain-"

"Don't fuckin' 'baby' me!" I yelled as I marched into our bedroom. "Don't you fuckin' 'baby' me, Dolla! FUCK YOU! I don't want to hear shit! I don't want to know how they got here or why they here! The shit don't matter!"

I grabbed the first pair of my pants that I saw. As I stepped into the leggings, the bitch had the nerve to touch me. I swung, landing on his chin and inches away from the baby's face, which I thought was a boy, but was so pretty that I couldn't tell.

Dolla looked at me like I was the worst person in the world. "Are you fucking serious? You gon' hit me with my baby in my arms?"

Nausea; that's what I felt as he protected this little motherfucker as if he was comfortable with its existence. That let me know that he had *been* known about these kids. He had built a relationship with these kids, and that shit broke me!

"I FUCKING HATE YOU! HOW COULD YOU DO THIS ME?"

I wanted to stop crying so bad. I hated looking like a weak bitch. I hated letting him know that he had hurt me because it gave him the upper hand, but this shit right here; this shit was the definition of wounded, agony, and suffering.

"Mama, we ready." Leave it to Brittany to come stand in the doorway fully dressed with Brandon's hand in hers.

When I went to grab my purse off of the bed, Dolla grabbed me, and I swung again. This time, he blocked me, causing me to wrestle to make contact with every part of his body. At that point, I honestly didn't give a fuck if I hit this baby. Call it what you want, but I really fucking didn't. The baby started to wail as Dolla attempted to shield it with one arm while he tried to hold me back with the other.

"Mommy, stop!" Brandon cried.

When I heard Brandon crying, I decided that if I wanted him to come with me with no hesitation, I needed to stop. So, I did, grabbed my purse and attempted to leave, but I was once again stopped by Dolla. He'd snatched me up and hemmed me up against the wall with the weight of his body. This baby was pinned between the both of us. I swear, God forgive me, but I wanted to snatch that baby out of his arms and throw it out the window.

"Just let me talk you," he begged.

As I heard Brandon's sniffles, my eyes went to my kids. I realized that since I was leaving their father, all they had was me. I couldn't go to jail for hitting this nigga or hurting this baby in the process, so as much as I wanted to, I didn't steal on his ass.

"Let me the fuck go," I growled. "If you want to ever see these kids again, I seriously advise you let me walk out *now*."

We stared at one another for a few seconds; his eyes refusing to let me go and mine refusing to stay. Then we heard Brittany's voice saying, "Daddy, please just let her go. Please?"

I saw so much hurt in Dolla's eyes as he finally let go of my arm, but I had no fucking sympathy for him. I walked out hoping that he was hurt just as much as I was so that maybe, *hopefully*, this nigga would die the same slow death that I was.

KENNEDY

"Aye, man. Yo' nigga crazy."

I rolled my eyes into the back of my head as I sat on Glen's couch watching as he laughed while locking the door behind Dre.

Though this situation was the death of me, as Dre raced towards me, she had the nerve to have a smile on her face. "It's good to see you," she said.

She looked me up and down... and then up and down again... and then up and down again. I knew that she was checking me out. She had only seen me in prison scrubs and a struggling ponytail; far from the shiny, flowing barrel curls from overseas, the designer maxi dress and sandals, and the beat face. Though it was the middle of the night, I had yet to change into something comfortable. For hours, I had been sitting on this couch, mourning both the loss of Ms. Jerry and King. The only thing worn or tired on me was my eyes. They held the residue of tears through lightly smeared make-up and pooling tears that had been constant in my eyes.

To Dre, however, I still looked a hundred times better than I did when I was locked up. I could see the shock and admiration in her eyes.

"Whatever," I hissed. "Don't talk to me. I'm mad at you."

When Glen chuckled, it was as if Dre finally realized that he was in the room. "Oh, hey, man. What's up? I'm sorry for barging in your house." Then she walked a few steps towards him with her arm outstretched. She shook his hand with sympathy in her eyes as she told him, "Sorry for your loss."

He gave Dre a contorted smile and said a dry, "Thanks," but then he added, "Sorry for your loss as well. I know how much she meant to you and Kennedy."

His words triggered emotions that I had only managed to get under control an hour ago. When Dre saw the oncoming of my hysterical cry, she rushed towards me, sitting beside me and attempting to put her arm around me.

But I swatted her arm away. "Don't touch me! I'm mad at you!"

"I'm sorry," she instantly apologized.

"I don't want to hear that shit! You should have told me!"

"I wanted to tell you in person. I knew I would see you soon-"

"I don't want to hear that shit! I'm so sick of people, who claim to love me so fucking much, keeping shit from me!"

Luckily, Glen and I had spent the last few hours venting to one another and sympathizing with one another. Though his father, Ms. Jerry's son, Henry, was only ten years old when his mother went to prison, they had a tight relationship, so his son, Glen, had grown close to his grandmother as well through calls and visits. Glen and I, as well as me and Henry, had gotten to know each other very well through conversations while I was locked up and even during visits when they visited on the same day as my people. Therefore, Glen was not looking at me like I was crazy while I spazzed out in his living room. He was actually looking at me with a lot of sympathy.

Dre was also looking at me with an abundance of compassion. I kind of felt bad. She had gone through a lot to surprise me, and I was giving her all this mouth. When she called Glen a few hours ago to give him her condolences for Ms. Jerry's death, she was shocked as shit that I had answered Glen's cell phone, because he had grown tired of answering it all day. I was surprised my damn self to learn that first, she was out of prison, and second, that my soon to be ex-husband had taken his Gangsta Boo ass over her house pointing guns and shit.

Dre came right over as soon as I gave her Glen's address.

"I'm sorry," she insisted again. "I meant well, I swear."

This time, when she put her arm around me, I let her, and I even lay my head on her shoulder, something I had done so many times while locked up. It still felt so damn comforting.

"How did you find out?" Dre asked.

"Glen called me."

Glen smiled at the tension that was leaving from between Dre and me. He gave us privacy, saying, "I'm going to bed.

Kennedy, I'll check on Kayla on my way up. Dre, try to convince her to get some sleep."

Dre watched Glen with the most peculiar smirk on her face as she watched him walk up the stairs. "What the hell you doin' over here?" she asked me once Glen disappeared onto the second floor.

I sighed heavily. "I called Henry because I wanted to give him my condolences and to make sure he was okay, and this is where he was, so I came over."

"Where is Henry?"

"He and his wife went home."

Dre glanced at her phone. "It's two in the morning, and you're still here."

Again I sighed. Having to retell this story was as painful as hearing the words out of King's own mouth again. "I...uhhh..."

The more I hesitated, the more concerned Dre became. "What? What happened?"

"I...uhhh... I found out that King and Si-Siren have a baby together. Elijah is his son."

The way Dre looked at me let me know that this shit was just as fucked up as it sounded, and that I wasn't overreacting. I wasn't being an overly-emotional woman. I had a right to feel every hurtful, deadly, and heartbreaking feeling that I was feeling.

"Damn, babe," she said with a heavy, exaggerated sigh. "That's.... that's-"

"Fucked up," I spat.

"Yea... What did he say?"

"Nothing. I overheard him talking to Meech about it. It sounded like Meech found out and then he told King-"

"So King didn't know?"

"No."

Dre looked a little relieved, but that tidbit of information didn't provide me with one ounce of relief.

"I can't believe they were fucking with each other and never told me. I went to jail for King. I took that case from him. I missed the first three years of my daughter's life for him. My daughter doesn't even fucking like me because she doesn't *know me.*" At this point, of course, those gawd damn tears were right back flowing down my face. "I did that shit because I just *knew* that my man was loyal to me, that the people that I was saving were more loyal than dogs to me. And it was all a gawd damn lie." I used the hem of my maxi dress to wipe my face, but it was useless. I wiped tears away, and others replaced them.

"So you're staying here?" Dre asked me, staring at my bags by the door.

"I wasn't. I didn't know where I was going because I can't be anywhere that King will find me. I can't talk to him right now.

But Glen insisted that I save my money on a hotel. Plus, I think he needs the company. He's grieving over more than just Ms. Jerry. His girl left him for some NFL third string player like two weeks ago."

"Damn. She trippin'. Glen got money too."

He did, but it wasn't the money that Dre and I were used to. Glen had learned from his grandmother's mistakes, so he never wanted a life in crime. He went to school, got his Bachelors and then Masters from Southern Illinois University. Now, at the age of twenty-six, he was a real estate broker. Ms. Jerry often bragged proudly that her grandson was worth nearly a million in his early career.

"I know, but it ain't fame," I told Dre.

Dre nodded in agreement and then changed the subject. "So you overheard King and then what?"

"I ran out."

"And you won't answer his calls?"

"I ran out of the house so fast that I left my phone, but I wouldn't have answered if he called anyway."

Dre chuckled and shook her head. "He's worried sick about you and Kayla, Ma."

I sneered and hissed, "I don't give a fuck. Let him worry."

CHAPTER TWO

KING

When I heard the doorbell ring, I jumped to my feet. All of the fatigue that I had been feeling from being up all night was gone all of a sudden. I ran to that door like one of those African track stars. I was praying that it was Kennedy. But if I was thinking clearly, I would have realized that Kennedy had a key, so she wouldn't be ringing the doorbell.

When I ripped the door open, I was completely let down when I saw Jada but was immediately concerned.

"What's up-"

She cut me off, snapping, "Where is Kennedy?"

As she forced her way inside, I let her. I felt bad for the kids, who looked tired as fuck.

As I closed the door, Jada sighed and ran her hands through her hair. I looked at the tears in her eyes, at how disheveled she and the kids looked, and I knew that she must have just walked out on Dolla.

"I still haven't found her," I admitted. When I heard the own sound of my voice, I felt sorry for myself. I sounded weak, guilty and broken.

"I need to talk to her," came from Jada's voice along with the sound of an oncoming cry.

Suddenly, Jada broke down. I mean, *down*. Her knees hit the floor, and she just wept into her hands. The kids looked at me for help, and I felt so bad for them.

"Aye, y'all go upstairs and sleep in the room next to mine, okay?"

Brittany weakly and sadly said, "Okay."

Brandon slowly followed her up the stairs. I waited until they were out of sight before I went to Jada.

I put my hand on her shoulder, and as soon as I squatted down beside her, she took her hands from her face and glared at me. "Did you know?" she asked.

"Know what?"

"About those fucking babies! *Did you know*?"

I was just as lost as she appeared to be. "What babies?"

She sucked her teeth and pushed me, causing me to fall back.

"Yo', what the fuck?!" I asked. "What's wrong? What babies?"

I thought maybe she was referring to Elijah, but she had said *babies*, so I was stuck.

"Those fucking babies that Dolla brought home tonight!"

Then, like a dumb ass, I looked at her with sympathy in my eyes. I was really feeling sympathy for Kennedy more so than Jada because watching Jada let me know that Kennedy was somewhere in this much pain. That shit broke my heart all over again.

I stood up, then wrapped my arms around Jada and brought her to her feet. She lay on my shoulder and cried in my arms. She had a nigga like me with tears in my eyes, man. I led her to the couch while hiding that shit, though.

"Now, what happened?" I had heard her loud and clear, but I still didn't believe that shit. Dolla really hadn't told me shit about no babies, so I was confused as shit.

"He came up with some babies."

"*Babiesss?*"

"Yes. Two. They looked the same damn age. They gotta be twins. I asked him whose babies they were, and he said they were his."

"Damn," was all I could say to that shit.

I had half a mind to call the nigga right then and there. I couldn't believe that he hadn't told me. But calling him would have only pissed Jada off, so I decided to wait.

"You really didn't know," she realized as she looked at the shock in my eyes.

When I shook my head, it was as if she got even madder. "This nigga been faking the funk with everybody. Lying ass bitch."

I couldn't say shit. After all that had happened the day before, and now this, I was thrown for a loop.

"Sorry for coming over here at this time of morning," she cried. "I drove around for hours after I left the crib. I couldn't even go to a hotel because I left ever dollar and debit card that I had at home. Plus, I just really needed to talk to Kennedy after that shit went down. She still won't answer her damn phone, though. Where the fuck is she? What happened?"

I sighed, saying, "Man…"

"What?" she urged.

I should have known better than to tell her the truth right at that moment. It wasn't the right time, but I'm a man, so as always, I picked the wrong fucking time to be honest. But, shit, I needed somebody to talk to about this shit.

"Meech came over here today and laid some shit on me…" I couldn't even look her in her eyes. I looked away from the awaiting look that she was giving me and stared at the carpet. "He said Eric ain't Elijah's daddy. He saw Eric and confronted him about not being in Elijah's life. Eric told him that he never even slept with Siren."

"Okay? What that got to do with Kennedy?"

"Well....Uhhh... He said that when he confronted Siren, she said Elijah was mine."

So, when Jada starting cracking up laughing, I knew that Dolla's stunt and lack of sleep had made the girl go psycho. I looked at her like she was a fucking psychopath, and when she saw no humor in my eyes, she stopped laughing.

"The fuck she mean he yours?" she spat.

Now she was dead ass serious. The tone of her voice had me scared as shit, as if I was talking to Kennedy, not her. I then realized how fucked up it was going to be when Kennedy and I had this conversation. My eyes went back to the carpet in shame.

"I used to fuck Siren back in the da-"

Phwap!

Jada had smacked the shit out of me so fast and so hard that it took me a minute to see straight.

"How fuckin' dare you?" I was trying to stop my ears from ringing as she jumped to her feet and continued to yell and snap at me. "After all she's been through? After all she's sacrificed for you! Gawd damn it, King!"

Then she walked out of the living room. "Brandon! Brittany! Get down here! We're leaving!"

I jumped to my feet. For some reason, seeing her walk out on me too seemed to only make shit worse. Plus, I had to look out for her and the kids for Dolla.

"Where the fuck you goin'?" I asked her.

"To my mama's house!" Then she started to call for the kids. "Brittany! Brand-"

I grabbed her. She acted like she wanted to fight me, but I was two feet taller than her and damn near a hundred pounds heavier than her. She probably got away with wrestling with Dolla, but over here, it was a no go. She was stuck in my grasp and couldn't move.

"Calm down and leave those fucking kids alone," I ordered as I pushed her ass back in the living room.

"Fuck you, King! I can't believe you!"

"I didn't know!" I promised.

"You knew you fucked her, though! You should have told Kennedy! You lying motherfuckers ain't said shit all these years! Fuck y'all! I hate you *and* Dolla! I'm leaving!"

When I stood in front of her, she didn't fucking budge.

"Yo' crazy ass ain't goin' nowhere. You ain't even got no money for a hotel."

"Then give me some!" When I laughed, she bit her bottom lip in anger. I ignored it and told her, "I ain't givin' you shit. I smell the liquor on your breath. You stayin' here."

As I walked out, she shouted, "Fine! But I ain't talkin' to yo' ass!"

I shouted over my shoulder as I headed for the stairs, "That's cool with me. The other guest room is ready whenever you are. Make yourself comfortable. Good night, Jada."

"FUCK YOU, *KING*!"

As I made it to the stop of the stairs, I laughed for the first time in a long ass time, felt like. "Love you too."

MARIA

"Fuck you, bitch," Brooklyn spat. "I ain't sayin' shit. Give me all the time you got... I want my lawyer and my phone call."

I chuckled with an emotionless shrug as I stood up from the metal table in the small interrogation room. "Suit yourself, Brooklyn."

I tried to appear as if I didn't give a shit, but I was steaming. This motherfucker knew when we arrested his ass in the middle of the night on Wednesday that he wasn't going to talk, that he was going to lawyer up. He'd toyed with us for an entire day, wasting our time, and for that, I hoped his dumb ass rotted away in prison.

I was done with this weak ass motherfucker. As I walked out of the room, a ball of disgust was trying to force itself out of my throat. I couldn't believe that these people were so blindly loyal to King that they would lose their life for him. First Kennedy, and now, Brooklyn.

Detective Jefferies looked at me with regret as he emerged from the surveillance room. "We've been holding him for over twenty-four hours. We have to let him make a phone call."

"Fine. Whatever. I don't give a shit," I mumbled as I ran my fingers through my red curls.

Detective Jefferies put his arm around me as he said, "Aye, don't be upset."

"What do you mean don't be upset? I'm pissed! I don't want *that* simple motherfucker. I want King!"

"We've been questioning him for hours. He's not budging."

"I know," I said, shaking my head in disgust. "Stupid motherfucker. He's facing damn near a lifetime and won't save his own ass. Ghetto piece of shit."

Detective Jefferies rubbed my shoulder soothingly as we walked towards my desk. "You've been here for two days straight. Why don't you go home and get some rest this weekend? I'll get Brooklyn booked."

Then it hit me, and I cringed. "Urgh. What if he gets bail? Who is going to be the judge Monday morning?"

"Greg Aguilar, so we're fine."

I relaxed. Greg Aguilar was a strict judge that hated thugs like Brooklyn, so I was sure that he wouldn't grant Brooklyn bail, leaving him to fight this case from the inside. Cases like this lasted a year, maybe even longer. I was sure that after sitting in jail for some time, the prosecutor could convince Brooklyn to take the immunity deal that would set him free as long as he testified against King.

As I gathered my purse and some paperwork, I told Detective Jefferies, "You're right. I should go home and get some rest."

He smiled and nodded. "See you Monday."

As I locked my desk and began to leave, I realized that I had nothing to go home to. It was a Friday. I should have been rushing home to my husband or to have a play date with my children. Yet, because of King, I was going home to neither. I had neither because of King and yet, he still hadn't paid for being the cause of me losing my husband and children. Everything I'd tried had failed, and rather than allowing Brooklyn's stubbornness to detour me, I was now even more determined to make King pay. King had done me dirty, so now maybe it was time for me to be even dirtier than he had been.

SIREN

I cringed as I looked at myself in the master bath of the guest bedroom that I had been staying in, in my own damn house. That London bitch had gotten me back and fucked my face clean up. My eyes were black, my lip was busted, and there were cuts all over my face from when London had clawed at it. The back of my head was tender to the touch. I even had a few knots on my head that made me look like Martin in the "Guard Your Grill" episode after he got his ass whooped by Tommy "The Hit Man" Hearns.

I took the alcohol and peroxide from the medicine cabinet to tend to the cuts on my face and many scraps all over my legs and arms from rubbing roughly against the pavement.

Meech hadn't even come home since I showed my ass at Aura Suites Thursday morning. Now, it was nearly Friday afternoon, and I hadn't seen or heard from him. I was expecting him to come home snapping on me, or at least for him to send me some angry text messages, but there was no sight of him. I knew that he was mad at me, but he hadn't even come home to check on Elijah. My heart sank as I wondered if he had run to London, but since he still hadn't drug me out of our home, I dared not drive over to her house to find out.

As I trashed the used cotton balls and returned the alcohol and peroxide to the cabinet, I sighed heavily. I had gone through a lot for two men that were off somewhere with other women that they loved way more than me, *if* they had love for me at all. King nor Meech gave a fuck about me. I had decided to let go of my obsession with King as soon as Meech found out about me and King's past, but maybe it was time for me to let go of my obsession with Meech as well.

As I lay on my bed, feeling the pain of every one of London's punches and the bullets that Jada tried to kill me with, I figured that it was time to cut my losses and just leave. I was fighting to stay with a family and crew that didn't even want me. It was time to leave before things got worse and I ended up losing the one person that loved me unconditionally; my son.

But where would I go, and how would I get there? Meech had completely cut me off after finding out about King. All of my bank and credit cards had been canceled. He'd moved all of his cash stash spots out of the house. The only thing the nigga was giving me was access to the crib and refrigerator. I knew that my days were numbered, and soon he would put me out, leaving me to fend for myself. I didn't know how to do that without my crew. Since I was in high school, I had been hustling with these people. I was too stubborn and full of myself to get a nine-to-five. Even if I wasn't, how could I get a job that would take care of me the way that I was accustomed to?

I needed to find a way to get *a lot* of money, take my son and get the fuck out of dodge… fast!

Chapter Three

KENNEDY

I didn't even know that Dre was in the room with me. I was staring aimlessly at the item in my hand, surprised that at that moment, I actually wished that I was back in prison. When I was released, I was happy. But in a matter of days, my life had gone from sugar to shit, and all I wanted was my happy life back; my old life, the one I had before I went to prison. However, as I stared at the item in my hand, I knew that I would never get that back.

My life would never be the same.

Like I said, I was so deep into my miserable thoughts that I didn't even know that Dre had come into the room, until I heard her voice ask, "You didn't hear me ringing the bell?"

"No. I'm sorry," I answered as she stared at my hand.

"What's that?"

I didn't even bother to hide it. I didn't even bother to keep it from her as she walked towards the bed, reached for it and snatched it from me.

"It's a pregnancy test," I told her as she stared at it.

"I can see that, and this motherfucker says 'pregnant.'"

I sighed deeply. "I know."

"Damn, you ain't been out of jail a whole month, and you already knocked up." Then she chuckled. However, when she saw that I wasn't laughing, she got serious, asking, "You not happy?"

I sucked my teeth as she sat on the bed. Her smell confused me. I smelled Escada Sentiment. It was a cologne, and it was pouring from her. The smell was amazing, but I wondered why the hell *she* had on *cologne.* Then I quickly realized that her stud ass wouldn't be caught dead wearing perfume.

Now, I was admiring her. Even in my misery, it was good to see her as a person and not a prisoner. She was wearing skinny fit men's, Levi jeans that rode on her ass, Jordan's and a wife beater that showed off her old tats and the new ones that she got while locked up. I admired her low cut, waves, and lining, which was fresh as fuck, as her green eyes looked at me with sympathy.

"No," I finally answered. "I'm not happy."

"Why not?"

"I don't want another fucking baby. I told King that."

Dre laughed. "You should have used a condom then or got on some birth control."

"I have an appointment to get on birth control next month. The nigga was supposed to pull out. He has been, but this had to have happened in Cabo. We were drunk as fuck, so he was probably sloppy with pulling out."

Dre watched me sulking and shook her head. "I don't see what's wrong with being pregnant by your husband."

"My lying ass husband you mean? My soon-to-be ex-husband you mean? Besides, I didn't want a baby even if he hadn't been caught up."

"Why not?"

"I just got out of prison. I want to live. I want to go back to college-"

"You can do that."

"No the fuck I can't. Not with two kids on my own."

Dre sucked her teeth and waved her hand dismissively. "You ain't gon' be on your own. You act like you're never going back to King."

"I'm not!"

"Bullshit," she smirked. "You spent three years trying to be back with this nigga, but you let some shit he did before he got with you run you away?"

My mouth dropped dramatically. "Are you fucking serious?! You act like this shit was a little white lie! This nigga was sleeping with one of the bitches closest to me. Siren and Jada was my circle. I didn't have any other friends. Siren and King never said anything. Shit, he could have been fucking her the whole time that he and I were together or the whole time that I was locked up!"

Just the thought brought back the same tears that I finally got to stop at around five that morning when I finally fell asleep.

Dre shook her head in disbelief. "I don't believe that. I don't think that nigga would do that. He loves you too much. Believe me, that nigga wouldn't jeopardize his 'queen' like that."

I looked at her with the same disbelief in my eyes. "Yea, and I didn't think he would ever lie to me or do anything to hurt me, but he did."

I could then hear the door of Glen's bedroom opening. As I heard him going down the stairs, I whispered to Dre. "Let's stop talking about it. I don't want Glen to know."

Dre looked at me sideways. "Why not?"

"I just don't."

She cocked her head to the side and watched me suspiciously. "Don't tell me-"

"No!" I insisted because I automatically knew what she was referring to. "Hell no. It's not like that. I don't want anybody to know because I'm not having it."

Dre's eyes bucked. "You crazy as hell! Are you fucking serious?"

"Dead serio- "

"Mommy, the movie went off! Can you put on Frozen now?" I tore my eyes away from Dre's judgmental eyes and looked at Kayla, who was standing in the doorway with her hands on her hips, looking at Dre with a serious mean mug as she asked, "Who you?"

Dre laughed at Kayla's smart mouth as she continued to embarrass me. "Where is my Daddy? I wanna go home."

Fuck my life, I thought as I ran my fingers through my hair. "I told you that we aren't going home."

Kayla cocked to the side; her eyebrows curled with confusion. "So we li' here?"

I sucked my teeth. "No."

"Then where we li'?"

"I don't know!" I should have known that yelling at her wouldn't make her attitude towards me any better, but shit, she was hitting me with too many questions that I didn't have the damn answers to. She was making my frustration worse.

Dre saw that, so she tried to help. Standing up, she told Kayla, "Aye, lil' mama, yo' mama not feeling too good. I'll go start the movie for you."

Dre walked towards Kayla, and when she went to hold Kayla's hand, Kayla snatched back and sneered, saying, "I 'on know you!"

Dre started cracking up laughing as I hid my face in my hands, fighting the urge to whoop her little ass.

I peered towards Kayla angrily, watching her sneer. Dre backed away from Kayla with her hands raised in submission. "This is definitely your daughter."

MEECH

Hearing the door of the office open made me jump out of my sleep.

I opened my eyes to see King and Dolla walking in and looking at me like I was crazy as I lay on the floor in front of the desk.

"Nigga, what happened?" King asked as he shut the door.

"You, ah ight?" Dolla spat hurriedly before I could say anything.

"I'm straight," I told them, standing to my feet. "I got too drunk to drive last night and just slept here. I didn't want to go to the crib no way, man."

"Damn," Dolla said, as he shook his head.

King looked at him like he had a lot of fucking nerve. "Really, nigga? You gon' be sleeping here too in a minute."

I watched the guilty look on Dolla's face and asked them, "What y'all talkin' about?"

King watched Dolla with a smirk as they both sat down in chairs against the wall. I sat on top of the desk, waiting for somebody to say something.

"The fuck is goin' on?" I asked when it took them too long to respond.

When Dolla kept avoiding our eyes, King said, "Fuck it." Then he looked at me with an expression that told me this shit was deep. "This nigga got Meagan pregnant and didn't tell nobody. She had twins. He been hidin' the twins since they were born. She died in a car accident, so the nigga had to take the babies home."

My mouth was on the floor when he said she had had the babies, but I damn near fell off the desk when he said that she died and that Dolla had to take them to the crib! I looked at Dolla, who was just holding his face and shaking his head. "Why the fuck you ain't say nothin' about her being pregnant, nigga?"

"I...I was just hoping that the shit would go away. I don't know..."

"What?" I asked him in disbelief. "Go away? At what point you thought that was gon' happen?"

"I don't know!" Dolla moaned. When King laughed, Dolla shot him a look of disbelief. "I know you ain't laughin'. You in just as much of a fucked up position as I am. You got a baby your girl didn't know about too! I can't believe you was fuckin' Siren and never told us."

King suddenly looked like he'd swallowed his own shit. Obviously, it was too soon to be cracking jokes about this shit. I had decided to look past the tension between us for the sake of Elijah and getting money, but the shit still wasn't funny to me.

"How you know already?" I asked Dolla as King continued to lower his head in embarrassment.

"He told me this morning after he called and told me that Jada and the kids are at his house."

Everyone went silent, and the tension in the room was becoming unavoidable, so I asked, "Aye, what the fuck are we gon' do about Siren? I need to go home to my son, but I can't tolerate Siren in the same house with me for much longer."

When King said, "I got a plan," I was happy as hell because I hadn't been able to think of shit we could do to get rid of Siren without the crew, our money, and organization suffering any repercussions.

As he ran the plan down to us, I was reminded why the three of us were able to build and maintain such a successful and prosperous empire. This nigga, King, was a genius. For some people, death wasn't enough punishment. Death is only redemption for the living, but for that person, it's not punishment because they don't feel anything; no pain, regret or sorrow, because they're dead. King's plan was a sure-fire way to get Siren out of our lives and make her pay while we continued with our lives making this money.

"Sounds good to me," I said once he was done.

"I'm game," Dolla was all too happy to say.

"Bet," King said with a nod as he reached for his phone, pushed a few buttons and waited.

Soon, the person that he was calling answered.

"Gustavo," King greeted. "I need a favor..."

DOLLA

"You sure about this, man?" King asked, with his eyebrow cocked.

I really wasn't, but I had to holla at Jada. We needed to talk. I hadn't called her since her crazy ass pointed that gun at me earlier that morning. I knew that this conversation had to be had in person; especially when I felt like shit that Brittany and Brandon weren't at home when I woke up that morning around the usual time that Jada and I would be getting them dressed for school.

This wasn't my life. Though I was indeed an ain't-shit-nigga, I was also very much a family man. Therefore, I was standing outside of King's house, ready to do what it took to get my family back. "Yea, I'm sure. I need to talk to her."

"With them with you?" King asked, pointing to the twins that I was carrying in their car seats.

"Where else they gon' go? My mama refuses to watch them because she mad at me for doing this dumb shit too. My lil' cousin watched them this morning for me, but she got her own kids to take care of. The nanny is coming to my crib to start tomorrow."

Still standing inside of his doorway leaning against the frame, King shook his head. "Then come back tomorrow."

I shook my head as well. "Nah. I want my kids at home with me *tonight.*"

Just as King opened his mouth to say something, I peeped Brandon running through the house behind him. "Aye, Brandon, come here! It's your Pops!"

As soon as he heard my voice, he stopped in his tracks, made an about-face, and ran towards the door.

I heard Jada's voice. "Brandon, where are you goin'?"

"Dad is at the door!" he yelled.

King moved out the way to let Brandon by as it looked like he was bracing himself for the bullshit. As soon as he moved out of the way, Jada barged through both Brandon and King, knocking them both down as she lunged at me with a knife.

"You gon' bring them motherfuckers with you?! You got a lot of fucking nerve, bitch!"

She was swinging at me with the knife in her hand, stabbing me with every swing! I had to turn my back to protect my face, heart, and the twins because she didn't give a fuck about any of that!

I could hear Brandon crying and King trying to get her to stop.

"Mommy, please! Stop! Don't kill Daddy!"

"Jada! What the fuck?!" King shouted. "Stop! That's enough! He's bleeding!"

She was still on top of me stabbing, slicing and screaming! "I hate you! I fucking hate you, bitch! Die! Just fucking die!"

She was so mad that even as small as she was, King had to struggle to get her off my back.

Just as the twins started to cry, I felt a vicious slice to my neck. "Arrrgh!"

"JADA!" King barked. "Stop this shit!"

"Arrrgh!" I heard Jada scream.

I didn't know what the fuck King had done to get her off of me, but it worked. I instantly sat the car seats down in the driveway and reached around the back of my neck. I could feel my flesh spilling out of the gash.

I spun around to see Jada wrestling to get out of King's chokehold. In the short time that we had been apart, I realized that I really did miss her. Laying eyes on her felt like I was seeing her for the first time. Even though she was spitting, screaming, kicking her bare feet, and crying, I looked at that girl and knew that my life wouldn't be same without her.

Brandon was in tears as he stood in the doorway watching. Brittany had come to the door as well and was looking at me like she hated me just as much as her mother did.

"Why the fuck would you bring them here?!" Jada screamed as she wrestled with King. "Where the fuck is they mama? Why she don't have 'em?! What? She a deadbeat bitch or something?

You cheated on me with a deadbeat, bum bitch that can't even take care of her kids?!"

"No, she's dead!" I yelled. "That's why she ain't got 'em!"

Jada had no remorse. She actually laughed and yelled, "Good! You next, bitch!"

She was fighting King like a lunatic. Her face was balled up like a pit bull as tears streamed down her brown skin and onto her chest that was exposed by a cami that was being pulled in every way as she wrestled with King.

"Dolla, just leave, man," King said through short breaths. Wrestling with Jada was wearing him out. Though she was so much smaller than him, she had the strength of an angry bull right about now. "Go before somebody calls the police."

"I ain't goin' nowhere! Jada just let me talk to –"

"FUCK YOU!" she spat.

"Then let my kids come with me!"

"Hell nah! They ain't goin' nowhere with you and them stankin' ass kids! They ain't my kids' brother or sister! Fuck them and FUCK YOU!"

"Dolla, nigga, leave!" King was getting frustrated and tired of wrestling with Jada; I could tell. "You bleedin' like a motherfucka anyway. You need to go the doctor, fam."

He was right. I could feel the blood streaming down my neck and onto my Saint Laurent tee. I tried to turn around to leave but couldn't tear my eyes away from the anger in Jada's eyes. That was exactly why I had never said anything about the twins until I was forced to; I never wanted to hurt her this much.

"Bruh!" King called me to get my attention, to get me to leave. Finally, I gave up, turned my back and made my way to my Viper. As I strapped the twins in, Jada tried desperately to free herself from King's grasp. Out of my peripheral, I could see her attempting to claw and kick her way out of King's grip—yelling and calling me every bitch and hoe in the book. Even as I drove away, I could hear her saying that she hoped that I died before I got to the hospital. Funny how I agreed with her. I was feeling emotional pain that I had never felt before, and it felt like the only way to make all of this better was if I died too.

CHAPTER FOUR

KING

It had been a week since Kennedy left. I was no closer to finding her than I was the day I read that note on the mirror in our bedroom. I had completely stalked her parent's house, but there was no sight of her. I had a hard time believing that Kennedy would go without contacting her mother or father for an entire week, especially after being gone for three years. But I knew Carla was more loyal to her daughter than me, so I left it alone.

"Okay," I sighed, after the last call. "Thanks."

"King..."

"Yes, ma'am?"

"Are you going to tell me what happened?"

I sighed and lay back on my bed. "I'll let her tell you, Carla."

"Tell me *something*," she insisted. "I'm worried."

"She's not in any danger, Carla. I promise."

"Okay," she reluctantly stated. "Do you think we should file a missing person's report or something?"

"No. She's using her debit card, so she's okay. She's just upset. I have an idea how to find her, though."

Again, she sighed. "Okay. Well, call me if you hear from her."

"I will. You do the same."

As I hung up, the same stomach-turning feeling was in the pit of my stomach. I felt like shit for the trouble I'd unintentionally caused. For days, I wracked my brain, wondering how I couldn't recognize my own son right before my eyes. I wondered why I was so ashamed of my rendezvous with Siren that I never told Kennedy. Back then, if felt like a good idea, but now I was feeling like that split decision that I made years ago was not just breaking my family apart, but my crew as well. Kennedy was gone, and though Meech was still fucking with me, the tension between us was thick as fuck. That nigga didn't trust me. His shadow wouldn't even come near me. I knew it would be a long time before he trusted me again, if he ever did at all. I was itching to meet my son officially, but I had to allow this plan to unfold first.

When my phone rang, as always, I hoped that it was Kennedy, but it was Brooklyn's baby mama. "What's up, Trina? What's the word?"

To make matters worse, after Jada went apeshit on Dolla, I got a call from Brooklyn's baby's mama telling us that Brooklyn had been arrested and was denied bail. She didn't know much else because Brooklyn didn't want to say too much over the phone. The buy he had arranged had gone totally wrong, and he felt like he had been set up. I should have known better than to allow him to sell to that buyer without me checking out the buyer first. I was so wrapped up in that fucking island and Kennedy that I gave Brooklyn more leeway than I usually would. She promised to call me today after she was able to visit with him, so I was expecting her call.

"I just visited with him."

"What's he talking about?"

"He said that the buyer was an undercover. The detective that arrested him is trying to give him immunity in exchange for him testifying against you. She got it out for you."

"She?"

"Yea. The undercover was a guy, but the detective over the case is some chick, Detective Maria Sanchez."

That had to be the same bitch detective that had been working with Siren. Suddenly, my head began to bang. For years, I'd run this empire with no hiccups, and now this bitch ass detective was trying to ruin everything and take food out of our mouths.

This bitch had to be handled.

"I'll look into that," I told Trina. "Did you tell him that the lawyer is working on another bail hearing?"

"Yea. And he told me to tell you not to worry about shit. He ain't sayin' shit."

"I know he's not. You need some money?"

"Brooklyn had a stash that will last us a while."

"As soon as you need something call me."

"Okay."

"Don't worry. He'll be out soon," I reassured her.

I hung up with so much pressure on me. Years ago, I hadn't been able to get Rozay out because he had three strikes, and I didn't have the pull then that I did now. That shit had fucked me up, and I swore that I would never let another member of my crew go down, so I had to get my nigga, Brooklyn, out.

After making another call, I waited for Sandra to answer. She was the wife of one of my buyers. She was also a clerk at the police station. Why she still worked a nine-to-five was beyond me. Her husband, G Money, said that she just loved her job. The universe works in mysterious ways though because I'd used her to help me a few times.

"Hey, King," she answered.

"Hey, Sandra. I need a favor."

"Anything for you. What's up?"

"I need all the information you can get me on a Detective Maria Sanchez in Vice."

"I got you."

SIREN

"Aye, Siren, the food is ready."

Meech stood in the doorway of my room, and I tried to hide my shock as I looked at him. "Okay. I'll be done in a second."

As he walked away, I admired how nice his ass looked in those Givenchy jeans. His bare back made my pussy cream.

Last Friday, Meech finally came home, and his attitude was totally unexpected. I thought he was going to barge into my room, drag me out of there by my feet and throw me on the curb with nothing. But instead, he was very cordial and had even been having conversations with me...although he still hadn't made mention of our relationship, and hadn't touched me. But we were still under one roof and doing things as a family, so there was hope.

I sashayed out of my room, down the stairs, and into the dining room in a tank, leggings and bare feet. It was a hot Friday afternoon in June, so even the central air had little effect on the eighty-degree sun that was beaming in through the bay windows.

Meech and Elijah were already sitting at the pub-style dining room table surrounded by barbecue ribs, hot links, burgers and hot dogs that Meech had been grilling most of the morning. He'd even made the sides himself: macaroni and cheese, a Caesar salad, and spaghetti.

"Hey, Ma! Look at all this food Dad cooked!"

My baby boy beamed at me from his seat on the leather bench next to Meech. Seeing his smile made the little remorse I felt for lying to Meech wither away. I felt bad for hurting him with my lies, but I had done it for a very good reason, and this sight before my eyes was that very reason. I might have been a snake ass bitch to some, but I had done it all for the happiness of these two boys sitting at this table. Elijah belonged to Meech, Meech belonged to me, and nothing else mattered beyond that. I had been allowing other people to matter more than them, but no more.

"Yea, your daddy showed out," I said with a smile, as I sat on one of the stools, the cold leather on the seat relieving me from the humidity between my big thighs.

I looked into Meech's face, and he was smiling so lovingly at Elijah.

Then he actually looked at me and winked, "Yea, daddy threw down for y'all."

I didn't know whether he was showing out for Elijah or whether he really meant that show of affection, but either way, it felt good. I relaxed and started to make my plate.

I started to rethink the extreme measures I was going through to get enough money to leave. Maybe things could actually work out eventually, and I wouldn't lose my family. But, *just in case*, I thought it was best that I continued to follow through with my plan to get money so that I had a nice stash spot, in case Meech's bipolar ass flipped out and decided to kick me out.

JADA

Unfortunately, King told me that the doctors were able to close Dolla's gashes with stitches. I was mad that he was alive, but I was about to kill him softly with the way I was about to come up without his ass.

After lying in bed for a week and crying my eyes out, I decided to get the hell out of the house. King told me that I could stay at his house since he had more room for the kids than my mother's house. I was for sure comfortable there, not having to explain to my mother what was happening, but the walls were starting to close in on me, especially after the tearful call I got from Dolla two days ago. He had just left the twins' mother's funeral. Through text messages that day, he had begged me to answer his calls, so I finally did. Her funeral had put so much into perspective for Dolla, and his sorrow was coming out in tears as he told me everything about Meagan.

When he was done, I was even more upset! Hearing their story made her a real person, not just someone in my mind that I knew nothing about. Even though she was dead, I now knew how long they had fucked around, how they met, what she knew about me, and it all just hurt so much more.

Some things are better left unsaid, and what is understood for damn sure doesn't always need to be discussed. I drank and cried for two days until I got fed up, remembered that I was a fucking G', washed my ass and got dressed.

The kids were with my mother for a week since they were out of school for the summer, and she had strict instructions not to let Dolla anywhere near them. King was in bed sulking over Kennedy, who I was mad as fuck at, by the way! I couldn't believe that girl hadn't called *me* of all people. She had a right to be pissed off. Her anger was my anger! We needed to be mad together! I needed her.

Anyway, since she was nowhere around to go get fucked up with me, I decided to go out with an old dip that had been calling for the last few days. I had never cheated on Dolla, but I flirted heavy with many niggas. I never had the courage to fuck any man besides Dolla, no matter what he did to me. He had broken my virginity and was the only man that had been in this pussy. But now that nigga was no longer "Daddy," and getting drunk and some good dick would make me feel a hell of a lot better about my man taking my heart out of my chest and running it over with his Viper.

"You a'ight?" Marcus asked me from the driver's seat of his Audi.

I looked at him and fake-smiled. In order to move on with my life, I had to fake the funk until that smile was real. I wasn't a punk bitch, so I refused to lie in that bed crying any longer. I was going to get my shit together, get me a job, hustle my damn self if I had to, get my own crib and show Dolla how much he really was losing when he lost me.

"I'm fine."

"No you not."

"I swear." This time, as I looked into Marcus' eyes, my smile was real because I was admiring how fine he was.

We met three years ago at a bar, but I never had the courage to actually go out with him, so he eventually stopped calling. When I met him, I was pissed off at Dolla because of his latest rendezvous, so Siren and I were drinking my misery away. He walked his thick ass into the door, and embarrassingly I couldn't take my eyes off of him. He was 6'3, a hefty two-hundred and seventy-five pounds, with chocolate skin and a full, long beard that he often played with. His apparel told me that he wasn't getting money like Dolla, but he wasn't broke either. After dancing with him and getting his number, I talked to him over the next few weeks. It was actually refreshing to talk to a man that wasn't so heavy in the game. I knew that he was in the streets somehow because he had a crib and car but never said anything about clocking in somewhere five days a week, but I liked talking to a nigga that had no association with Dolla or the crew. Plus, he moved around from here to Miami, so from what I knew, he didn't know anything about the squad. Me and

Marcus' conversations were about life, not dope, drops and collecting money. I liked that shit.

"Where you wanna go?" Marcus' voice, along with his hand on my bare thigh, brought me out of my trance.

I'd worn another pair of my extremely short shorts, but these were denim, along with a lace halter top that tied behind my neck. Of course, I'd paired the outfit with a pair of heels that made my ass look like a thoroughbred. I'd even worn one of those waist cinchers to hide my pudge and accentuate the fuck out of my hips. Then I decided to be different and wear my extensions in an updo that brought the features out of my dark, round face. I'd beat my face to death too. Then I tiptoed past King's bedroom so he wouldn't see how I was dressed, jumped in my Range Rover and met Marcus at his place.

"Let's go to LaMelle's," I responded. "I want to drink... a lot."

He smiled, his dimple dancing in the darkness of the car. "Cool."

DOLLA

I hadn't been right since Meagan's funeral two days ago. Shorty didn't even look the same as she lay in her casket. The collision from her accident had totally mangled her face; so much so that I barely recognized her.

I didn't expect for that funeral to affect me the way that it did. But as I sat staring at her unrecognizable body, I wondered what part I played in her death while knowing what part I had played in Jada's emotional death. She hated me. That was confirmed every time she stabbed me with no remorse at all. She wanted me to die because she felt like she was dying, and I hated to be the person that made her feel such pain. I was her man. I was the man of our household. I was supposed to protect her and my children from hurt, but as I watched their hurtful eyes look at me as I drove away from King's crib that day, I knew I had failed.

I left Meagan's funeral knowing that I had to do whatever I had to do to make things right with my girl and my two oldest children. It was illogical to think that we could ever be a happy family including the twins, but crazier things had happened.

No matter my many attempts to call or go by King's house without the twins, Jada was not trying to hear me. We'd only managed to have one conversation after I begged her to talk to me after Meagan's funeral. I told her everything about Megan. But my honesty only seemed to piss Jada off even more.

I figured that I needed to give her some time to calm down. Maybe after the dust settled and she missed the nigga she had been with all of her life, she would come back to me with my kids.

Until then, a nigga was gonna drink his sorrows away. I decided to go to this new bar, LaMelle's that one of my homeboys had just remodeled on 87th Street. I heard that it had been cracking on Friday nights. I was on my way all alone. I was told that LaMelle's had a sick ass patio, and since it was about seventy degrees at night, I planned to sit back there with a drink and some loud.

As I pulled my Viper up to the parking space, I watched as thot after thot struggled in six-inch heels to get inside of the club. The club had a huge bay window, so I could see how packed the club was.

Imagine a nigga's surprise when I noticed a fat 'ol ass that I had been hittin' for the last couple of years boo'd up with some big ass dude handing her a drink. I couldn't believe that Jada was out with the rest of these thots when she had a family back at the crib! I knew what she was going through, but the shit she was on was reckless as fuck. The streets talked, and I owned these motherfucking streets. Everybody knew who she was and who her nigga was. I didn't give a fuck if I had brought two babies home; that bitch knew better than to be outside with some random ass nigga like she was one of these regular bitches.

After all these years, I had never seen or heard of Jada being with another man. I hadn't even had a gut feeling or thought that she would be with some other nigga. But as I jumped out of my car and ran towards that club, it was very evident that Jada was so hurt that she was going to do anything to make the pain that I'd caused go away.

I tore through the door of the club, alarming the bouncers, who I knew were on my heels. I flew through the crowded club towards those little ass denim shorts and thick thighs by the bar standing way too close to that square ass nigga. I had knocked a few motherfuckers over and spilled many drinks on my way, but I didn't give two shits.

As soon as I was in arm's reach, I snatched Jada's ass up before she even saw me coming!

"Bitch, you out here doin' dicks already?!" I yelled as I hemmed her up against the bar and made her drop her drink. The glass crashed to the floor.

Immediately, the tight crowd in front of the bar was now looking at me like I was the one that wasn't shit. Even some drunk bitches tried pulling me away from Jada, but that shit didn't faze me. All of my attention was on Jada, who didn't know what the fuck was going on at first. As soon as she saw my face, the happy, drunk haze that was previously on her face was gone and the snarl that she had been giving me was back.

"Fuck you, bitch!" she spat as she swung on me.

Her punches didn't even faze me. I was so mad that I didn't even feel that shit. I grabbed both of her arms even tighter and brought my face closer to hers. "Nah, fuck you! Why the fuck is you in here dressed like a hoe all on this punk ass nigga?!"

I was surprised that the bouncer hadn't stopped me yet. Yet, usually, when a nigga was catching his bitch up in the club, the bouncers thought that shit was funny and let it ride. Shit, somebody was probably recording this, and it probably would be viral on social media by morning. I didn't give a fuck, though. Jada was the one that was going to be embarrassed.

But right now she didn't give a fuck. She growled right back at me like she wasn't doing shit wrong. "You got a lot of fucking n-"

"Fuck that!" I barked. "You won't even let me get my kids, but you out here fucking like a slut!"

"Fuck you! Go home and feed them no-mama-having-ass babies, bitch!"

I instantly let her go and aimed to smack fire from her ass. She didn't even flinch, though. She squared up with me, and I knew then that our love was turning to hate real fucking quick.

Before we could exchange blows, the lame ass nigga that she was with came towards me. I immediately reached for my piece in my back. Everyone screamed.

"Oh God!"

"Jesus!"

"Run!"

That's when the bouncer stepped in and dragged me out of the club before I could pull the trigger.

CHAPTER FIVE

JADA

I was so fucking embarrassed, but not by these ratchet ass bitches that were looking at me with shade on their faces. Half of these bitches probably wanted to fuck Dolla, and they could have his ass! I was embarrassed because Marcus was standing his fine ass next to me, looking at me with a thousand questions on his face.

As the lights turned off and the music came back on, I leaned into Marcus and apologized. "I'm so sorry. That was my baby's father. He is crazy as fuck."

"I see that. He almost got it, though."

I snickered, not bothering to tell him how he was lucky that that bouncer stopped Dolla from putting several holes in his ass and anyone who got in his way. As I peered out of the bay windows of the club and saw Dolla's Viper sporadically pulling away, I figured we needed to get the hell out of there before he came back with backup.

"Let's go...." I paused as I rubbed his Ralph Lauren covered chest. "...to your place," I purred.

His eyebrow rose, and a sexy smirk appeared amongst his dimples. "Word?"

I licked my lips, suggestively. "Word."

"Let's go then."

He grabbed my hand and led me towards the exit. I was the happiest I had been in a long time. I was about to get me some dick! Yaaaas! Nothing like new dick and laying under a big, strong man to make your problems go away... even if only for a few hours. I didn't even give a fuck if I never heard from Marcus again afterward either.

"You smoke?" he asked when we hopped into his Audi.

"Yep. You got some loud?"

He chuckled sarcastically. "Of course, I got that Keisha."

"Then roll up."

Before starting the car, he reached into his console and pulled out a Swisher. As he broke it down and started to roll the blunt, I checked my phone. I was hoping for a text message from Kennedy, but there was some weird, random ass text message from Siren, bragging about Meech finally being nice to her again. I didn't know why that crazy ass bitch kept talking to me like we were besties!

Then a barrage of messages started to come in from Dolla. He was cursing me the fuck out, and it made me smile to know that I had finally showed that nigga how hurtful it was to see the love your life with somebody else. He was calling me so many nasty, slut bitches that I didn't want to fuck the night up any further by responding to him, so I turned the phone off just as Marcus was handing me the blunt and a lighter. He then turned the engine, and a Bando Jonez song filled the air in the car.

♪ *All the rain keeps falling*
And these hoes keep calling
Uh
Ah, all these raindrops falling on my window
Got me wishing that we did the things we didn't do
And right now I wanna sex yoooou, baby ♪

We pulled off in silence, smoking and letting the words of the song put us in the mood. I had had a few nervous jitters before, but the loud was chasing them away. I had nothing to be nervous about anyway. Dolla had been getting his; it was time that I stopped being some dumbass, loyal, ride or die chick and get mine.

♪ Has anybody sexed you lately
Got all these hoes calling asking me to come through
(Asking me to come through)
What they don't know
Is it all just make me wanna call you, you
You you you you you you you you you
And ask you if I can sex yoooou, lady ♪

****

Biiiiitch, when I say that man fucked the shit out me! Chilllle! Yaaaaaaaas!

My frantic ass had taken every article of clothing off as he kissed me and then ate this pussy so good that that beard tickled my ass as he munched on it. When I squirted, that shit turned him on, and he quickly stripped as well, revealing a body full of tattoos. He was chiseled and defined like Dolla, but his football build was hard, and he was using all his massive strength to force this ass back on his dick with perfection.

"Shit! Oh! My! God!"

He had me on all fours in the middle of his bed giving me *all* the business.

"Gawd damn!" I wanted to ask this nigga to wait a second. My pussy was only accustomed to one nigga who *was* well-endowed, but, gawd damn, this motherfucker had a big ass dick and knew how to use it!

"Awwwwww! Oh my God! I'm cumminnnnnnng!" A bitch had tears in her eyes! I wanted to be a G and throw this pussy back, but fuck that! My back couldn't even stay arched. That hump kept forming, as I tried to adjust to his dick, and he kept pushing it back down.

"Unt uh, arch that back, baby. You don' kept this pussy from me for too long, and I want it all."

He grabbed my waist and got even deeper into this pussy. I was so glad that he was hitting it from the back because he couldn't see the way my eyes were squinting from pressure that I wasn't used to and the fucked up faces that I was making.

"Yes, Marcus!"

"That's it," he grunted. "Say my name, baby."

"Marcus!" Shit, I would have spelled his name if he asked me too! Gawd damn!

This nigga was straight *fucking* me. This was some deep stroking, hair pulling, ass slapping, gut banging, waist gripping, toe curling *fucking*! I was sweating from head to toe. My pussy was begging for mercy. I wanted him to stop, but I wanted more at the same damn time.

"Damn, you fuckin the shit out of me," I whined with heavy breath.

A bitch wanted to cry! Yaaaas!

"Mmm humph," he said as he smacked my ass. "Wish you would have gave this motherfucker to me a long time ago, don't you?"

"Yes," I nearly cried. "Yes!"

****

I fell asleep? Damn.

My eyes fought to adjust to the darkness. I could feel that I was still naked. My now sober mind raced to recall where I was. I then remembered that I was in Marcus' bed. I looked over, and he wasn't there. I heard noise outside of the closed door so went to get up, but as I tried to move my arms and legs, I couldn't.

"What the fuck?" I muttered.

Frantically, I attempted to move my arms and legs but felt something cold and metal around my wrists and ankles, preventing them from moving.

I started to scream. "MARCUS! WHAT THE FUCK?!"

What kinda freaky shit is this nigga on?

"MARCUS!!!"

As I heard the bedroom door opening, I was getting madder, kicking and throwing my arms and legs as if that was going to get me out of these, what felt like, cuffs.

"What the fuck is this shit?! MARCUS!"

The door flung open, and the light suddenly came on. I quickly looked at my wrists and ankles, and, indeed, I was handcuffed.

"What the fuck, Marcus?!" I looked at him like he was crazy. I wondered why he was just standing in the doorway calmly, instead of rushing to free me. "Why are you just standing there?! Let me out! What kind of freaky shit are you on?"

His voice was so calm that it frightened me more than the handcuffs. He stood there with a bare chest and jeans, and even barefoot. "I'm not letting you out..." With every word he spoke as he walked towards me, my heart beat rapidly with worry and fear. "... until you call your nigga and tell him I want three-hundred thousand dollars in exchange for me letting you go."

When he saw the look in my eyes, he continued to persuade me, "Aye, three-hundred thousand dollars is nothing to yo' nigga. Just call him and this shit will go easy and you won't get hurt."

You gotta be fucking kidding me! How does he even know Dolla?

"Are you fucking serious?" I sneered.

As he reached into his pocket and pulled out my cell phone, I knew that he was very serious.

"Real serious, Ma. Now give me your code."

He had turned my phone back on, but it was locked.

"I'm not giving you shit!"

"C'mon. D-"

I cleared my throat, aimed and hocked a fat loogie right on his face. Instantly, he aimed and punched me dead in my stomach.

"Uggh!" I immediately turned my head in order not to choke on the vomit that spilled from my throat.

"Don't fucking play with me, bitch! Just do what the fuck I said! What's the code?!"

Vomit was all over my face and in my hair as I spat, "Fuck you!"

There was no way that I was calling Dolla. I hated him, but I wasn't about to set him up. I was no Siren-type bitch. I didn't know this nigga's angle. He said he wanted money, but obviously, I didn't know this motherfucker like I thought I did. He could be trying to kill Dolla. *I* wanted to kill Dolla. His blood was on *my* hands, not this nigga's.

Fuck this nigga!

I cringed, preparing for him to hit me again, but instead, he sucked his teeth, shook his head and stormed out of the room, after turning the lights back off and shutting the door.

I hope he kills me.

I really did. At the point, I welcomed death. In so little time, my life had gone down the drain, and at the moment, it looked like there was no fixing it in sight. All of my best friends had turned on me; Siren, Dolla, and even Kennedy. None of them were there for me like I had been for them. I no longer had the family that I once had. I would have to start all over with a broken heart. I couldn't even pick a new nigga right because I didn't see this shit coming from Marcus at all. I would have rather died than live on with this excruciating feeling in my heart.

SIREN

My phone rang at about two in the morning. I wasn't sleeping, though. It was a hot Friday night. I should have been outside with my nigga, but Meech wasn't back to claiming me yet. I should have been outside with my girls, but now that Meech knew that King was Elijah's father, I wouldn't dare let him catch me phony kicking it with Kennedy. And Jada?

Well...

"Hello?"

"She ain't goin'," Marcus spat.

I sucked my teeth as my eyes rolled into the back of my head. "Figures." I knew Jada would be on some ride or die shit. "Fuck that bitch up and make her do what you say!"

"I did! She still won't."

"Then *you* call him. Go through her phone."

"I can't. Her phone was off. When I turned it on while she was sleep, it was locked. She won't give me the code."

"Sleep? She actually fucked you?"

"Yea," he chuckled. "You thought she was too wrapped up in that nigga to give that pussy up, but she did. I guess they into it or some shit. He came in the club and everything, trying to fuck her up. She snapped on that nigga and stayed."

Damn.

I wondered what the fuck was going on. Even though I was acting like the bitch was still my bestie, I knew that she didn't fuck with me so wouldn't give me any tea on her or Dolla. This shit was crazy, though. No matter what stunt Dolla pulled, Jada always stuck by that nigga, which was why I had come up with a plan to use her to get the money I needed to put away in case Meech kicked me out.

Marcus was a nigga that Jada flirted with for years but never really fucked with. When we met him at the club, I thought he was cute and actually wanted him for myself, but he was feeling Jada. So as she would show me his flirtatious messages and dick pics, I memorized his number. I knew she wasn't going to fuck him so I figured I could play with the nigga too. We fucked around once or twice, but I knew through Jada that they were still talking. Obviously, the nigga wasn't shit, and I could tell that he got his money a certain way. So, a few days ago when I knew I needed to get some money, I called him and told him my plan of using Jada to get some coins to leave comfortably with Elijah if Meech put me out. However, it seemed like I was closer and closer to a state of forgiveness, so maybe I didn't need this money at all.

"What am I supposed to do?" Marcus asked. "You got the niggas number, right?"

"Yes, but she is going to know it's an inside job if you already have his number, dumbass," I spat.

I shook my head. This nigga could fuck like a dream, but he was as dumb as a doorknob.

"I can't just let her go. She knows me. Plus, I want this money."

"Do what you have to do to make her give you that code, and then kill her! Shit, I don't give a fuck."

I really didn't. Jada was liable to tell my secrets any day now. It would be much better for me and my position in Meech's life if I killed the one person that knew everything about me.

"Kill her? Nah, I ain't no killa, ma. I jack niggas; that's it."

My head fell into my hands. "You goofy motherfucker. Didn't you just say she knows you? You think, whenever you get her to call, that they gon' give you the money and then just let it be? They gon' come looking for you."

He sighed. "You right."

"Bet."

Then I hung up, used the remote to turn off the TV and laid down to get some sleep, thinking, *Dumb motherfuckers. They'll probably both die tonight.*

KENNEDY

I was sitting at Glen's computer crying. I had checked my emails and saw a message from the wedding photographer with a link to our wedding pictures. It was so crazy to me how I was so happy just two weeks ago, and now I was miserable.

As soon as I heard Glen coming down the stairs, I wiped my face and closed the website. Ms. Jerry's funeral had been the day before, and I knew that he was tired of crying himself and seeing me cry, so I put on a big girl smile when I turned to look at him, but my smile quickly turned into admiration. He was entering the den with no shirt and basketball shorts. He was sweating and breathing heavily, which was causing a feeling inside of me that only King had been able to cause for years.

"You okay?" I asked him.

"Yea. Just got done working out in the garage. What's wrong with you?" he asked as he came towards me.

"Nothing," I lied, shaking my head quickly, but he knew better. He walked up to the desk and leaned on it next to me as I acted as if I was putting all of my attention on an email.

Then he put his hand on my chin and brought my eyes up to his.

Gawd damn, this nigga fine. Ooo, Lord.

For some reason, Glen just made me weak. He was a smooth tan complexion, with a low cut fade and crisp lining. His features were dark, which gave him an exotic, Dominican look, and he had a slim-fit build that gave him an athletic appeal. He was shorter than King, standing at only 6'0. His swag was mature and different from what I was used to, which made his personality way sexier than his looks.

Sometimes I thought it was the absence of King that just had me drawn towards Glen. Then I thought it was the pregnancy hormones. So, I had been ignoring my attraction towards him for the last few days.

Shyly, I tore my eyes away from his. Then he took his hand and wiped away the residue of tears that I had missed. Just as he was doing so, there was a knock on the front door and then it opened so quick that as Dre entered, she looked as if she had caught me and Glen in a compromising position.

I kinda felt like she had. For some reason, I felt guilty, so I jumped to my feet. "Hey, Dre. I'm ready."

"Where are you going?" Glen asked.

"Dre is taking me to get another cell phone. I need to at least call my parents."

I was honestly skeptical about calling my mama because King had her wrapped around his finger. I figured I'd call her anonymously or something. Plus, I really wanted to call my father. We had just made amends. I didn't want to mess that up by disappearing.

Glen nodded and actually looked like he was hesitant to see me go. For a week, we had been attached at the hip, helping one another mourn our losses. We had become kinda used to each other.

I smiled. "I'll be right back," I told him.

"Where is Kayla?" Dre asked.

"She's sleep. Glen, can she stay here until we get back?"

"Sure thing, babe."

Babe?

I actually got goosebumps. To force myself to focus on something else besides his beautiful eyes, I rushed towards the couch, grabbed my purse, and walked towards the door, attempting to keep it cute and not fall on these weak knees.

As soon as Dre followed me out of the house and closed the door behind her, she started grilling me. "Babe?"

"Don't start, Dre," I warned forcing back a smile.

"Heffa, are you blushing?"

"No!" But I was!

"You *like* that nigga!"

"No, I don't!" I fussed. "I don't know shit about liking nobody but King."

I really didn't. That nigga was all I knew, which was why I had served that time for him. And what did he do? Deceive me!

"Fuck King," I muttered as I moped towards Dre's mother's car and got into the passenger seat. I avoided Dre's eyes as she climbed into the driver's seat. She started the engine while looking at me in shame. As soon as the car came on, Usher's voice filled the car.

> ♪ If there's a question of my heart, you've got it
> It don't belong to anyone but you
> If there's a question of my love, you've got it
> Baby, don't worry, I've got plans for you, yeah ♪

"Urgh! Turn that off!" I didn't even wait for Dre to turn off the radio. I quickly turned it off myself as she looked at me as if I was losing my mind.

"That's the song that played at our wedding," I explained.

Her judgmental glare was then replaced with sympathy. "What you gon' do, Kennedy?"

"About?"

"About King! You can't hide forever."

"I know," I whined. "But I can't face him, Dre. That nigga hurt me so bad that it's a wonder I haven't lost it. I don't want to live with this feeling in my heart. I can't."

"I know, ma, but you can't hide here forever. At least go get a hotel and call King. You got money. You don't have to stay here."

A skeptical grin spread across my face as I glared at Dre. "Are you jealous?"

"Of what?"

"Of Glen!"

"Hell nah!"

But then she started to blush, so I knew it was a lie.

"You think you the only nigga that can crush on me besides King?" I teased as I playfully poked her stomach.

"Whatever," she said as she swatted my arm away. "I just don't want you making matters worse. King find out you over here with a nigga and he gon' tear the city up."

"I know, but I have to stay here so he won't find me. I'm not strong enough yet. He'll romance his way back into my life, and I'll be playing stepmom to him and Siren's baby." Just the thought made me gag. As I stared sadly out of the window, my eyes fell on Glen's house. My eyes caught the sight of him looking out of the window at me. He smiled, and he actually made the sadness go away. "I can't leave," I told Dre as I stared at Glen. "I'm not ready yet."

CHAPTER SIX

MEECH

♪ *Bitch you guessed it, walkin' around with extra in my pocket*
Bitch, you next to us. Why the fuck are you next to us?
Bitch, you should come test us
I seen what you rockin' and bitch you can't dress with us
Seen what yo' bitch looked like
And nigga, I wasn't impressed or nothin' ♪

I was sitting in my ride outside of London's mama's crib. I had been out there for about thirty minutes, waiting for her to come out. I knew her work schedule, so I was expecting her to emerge from the crib on her way to the bus stop to make it to work in the next hour. She still hadn't been answering my calls. In fact, I think she blocked a nigga because my calls were going straight to voicemail. So, I had to result to stalking.

Right on time, London came barging out of her front door in a rush.

"Oh hell no!" she spat as soon as she saw me.

I figured London would lose her fucking mind the moment she saw my face, but I had given her enough space. She had to hear me out. I jogged up behind her as she power-walked up the street towards the bus stop.

"Hold up."

"Nah! Ain't no 'hold up'! Fuck you and that crazy ass bitch you fuckin' with!"

"I'm not fuckin' with her!"

She stopped so abruptly that I nearly collided with her. When she finally turned around to look me in my eyes, a nigga got weak and shit. I really liked shorty. I *really* did. It had only been a little over a week since I saw her face, but now, watching as her crinkled dreads fell in her face, it felt like forever since I had laid eyes on her.

I'm in trouble, I thought to myself as I smiled at her.

"Don't you fucking smile at me!" she spat. "Ain't shit to smile at!"

"I'm sorry. I couldn't help it. It's good to see you, ma."

She waved me off. "Don't give me that shit! I wasn't playing when I told that bitch she can have you!"

This time, I smiled on the inside instead, remembering the sight of London's beating on Siren's face when I got home. "But I don't want her."

"But she lives with you, right?" she asked folding her arms, waiting for an answer. "Right?!" she pressed after it took me too long to open my mouth.

I sighed and ran my hand over my head nervously. "Yea, she does, but-"

"But nothing!" she snapped as she started to march away.

I stopped her, though, running in front of her and blocking her path, my eyes begging her to listen to me. "I left her right before you and I met. I haven't touched her since I met you."

"But she lives with you! That's what's wrong with you niggas. Housing these hoes that you don't want no part of but you're too much of a punk to make the bitch leave! Then you expect her to act like a 'roommate.' No, that bitch got feelings for you! And as long as she got a foot in the door, hell, a pinky toe, she thinks she's your woman!"

I blew breath as my shoulders shrunk because, hell, she was right than a motherfucker. There was so much to the story that I couldn't tell her as we stood in the middle of the sidewalk.

"I'm trying to get her out. It's complicated, ma."

"It's always complicated!" she snapped as her arm flailed. "Just move out of my way, Meech!"

"Please-"

"NO!" The tears in her eyes surprised me as she continued to yell, "Just leave me alone! I don't want to be involved with anything 'complicated'! I don't deserve that!"

Again, she was right; she didn't deserve the pain in her eyes, and I hated that I was the nigga that put it there. I hated that what happened that day at Aura Suites had washed away how much I'd shown her how I felt for her. She didn't even see that I hated myself for making her feel the frustration that she was feeling as she marched towards the bus stop. I hated to watch her leave me again, but that damn sundress was giving me a hell of a view to mourn.

KING

I was sitting in the crib in the darkness. Though it was a sunny, Saturday morning, I had the curtains drawn in my bedroom. I reached over to Kennedy's side of the bed as I lay face down on the pillow, wishing that I could feel her phat ass or thick thighs underneath my hand instead of the cold sensation of her side of the sheet that hadn't felt her body heat in so long.

I couldn't believe that I was back here; missing my baby. I couldn't believe that it was, once again, my fault that she was gone.

I had used every outlet I had to find her, but nothing came up. I had even done a people search on Ms. Jerry to find every address associated with her so that I could find out when her funeral was, but it was a shot in the dark. Ms. Jerry and her husband had gone to prison so long ago that every address associated with them was now occupied by people that had no idea who they were, besides her son. So, I had gone to Ms. Jerry's son's crib to see if I saw any sign of Kennedy, but I hadn't. As I sat there day after day, I figured that I must have gotten there too late, after Ms. Jerry's funeral. I never saw a limousine or a stream of visitors.

I had learned that Ms. Jerry's son, Henry, had some high position in the Mayor's office. With the shit that I currently had brewing, I couldn't afford to go through his crib with guns to his face asking about Kennedy, so I had to cut my losses there. But as I saw that nigga coming out of the crib, I figured she wouldn't be held up in his house anyway. He was old as fuck with a wife that wouldn't let Kennedy's pretty, phat ass lay up around her husband.

I was lost, and above missing the fuck out of my queen and princess, I hated feeling fucking lost. I was King. I figured out everything, all except when it came to losing Kennedy. She had finagled her way into doing that time for me, and she had finagled this shit too. No matter how young she was, no matter how much I tried to keep her sweet and naive, she wasn't so dumb that she couldn't figure out how to make me feel completely helpless.

I groaned as I felt my phone vibrating on the pillow next to me. I stopped hoping that it was Kennedy days ago when my phone would chime a notification. I was right not to get my hopes up. It wasn't her, but the notification was something else that I was looking forward to. It was a picture message from Trina, saying, "This is Detective Maria Sanchez's information." It included the detective's home address, phone number, and a picture. I stared at the picture for only a second, not expecting to know her at all. But those eyes reminded me of a night I had with a little Latin thang ten years ago.

"Ooooh shit."

It was her, and I knew it. I didn't remember her name being Maria, but I did recall that night being hazy as fuck. I was drunk as shit and only remembered fucking some young pussy in my truck and then dodging her calls after that.

Why the fuck would she have it out for me? I wondered.

The answer didn't matter, however. That bitch was as good as gone.

JADA

"Arrgh!" My neck snapped to the left as Marcus' fist made contact with my jaw yet again.

"Just unlock the fucking phone, damn! You willing to die for this nigga? 'Cus I'mma kill yo' ass for fuckin' up this lick for me!"

Marcus was straddling my naked body. All night he refused to give me one article of clothing or to even cover me with the blanket. He thought that blasting the air would also convince me to give him the code. But neither the cold nor his beatings were making me budge. I was even lying in my own piss since he refused to even let me free long enough to use the bathroom.

But now, I was tired, cold, and sick. I could hardly feel anything as I remained handcuffed while he tried to beat that code out of me.

When my phone began to ring, my heart sank. I knew that it was my mother calling me again. She had been calling all day. I knew that she was worried because I was supposed to pick up the kids that morning, but Marcus refused to answer so that I could soothe her worry because he didn't trust me not to give him away.

As my tired eyes looked into his angry ones, it was as if a lightbulb went off in his head. He hopped up from the bed and went into the drawer. My heart began to beat rapidly as I feared what would happen next. Then my fears were confirmed. His hand emerged from the drawer with what looked like a gun, but what I soon recognized as a taser. My eyes grew big as he walked right up on me and pressed it against my chest. With no warning, he fired! My body went stiff as a board. My muscles and nerves were no longer functional. What was fucked up was that I was completely aware of every pain and awful feeling that thing was jolting through my body.

The electricity that shot through my body only lasted for a few seconds, but it felt like hours before it finally went away, my body went into a desperate relaxation, and I spat out, "FUCK!"

It didn't kill me, but that was a pain that I never wanted to feel again. I knew it as my tears formed in my eyes for the umpteenth time.

"You gon' give me the code?"

"Fuck y-"

Zap!

Again, he tased me. I wanted to yell out but, again, no muscle in my body could move as the pain in my chest sent shock waves through my body.

The seconds felt like days until it was over, and I could do nothing but lie there, unable to move my head and wishing that that damn taser gun actually had shot bullets into my chest instead of electricity.

"Just give me the fucking code," Marcus begged.

He was tired… and I was tired too.

"0-4-2-4-2-1-3."

DOLLA

Jada had been calling me all fucking day, but I had no words for her motherfuckin' ass.

Fuck that bitch!

"Is that her again?" my mother asked as I shoved my phone back into my pocket.

"Hell yea," I spat. "Fuck her."

My mother smacked my leg as she rocked Lil' Brandon back and forth. Bianca was lying on my lap sleeping.

"Watch your mouth," my mother told me.

"I'm sorry, ma, but she pissed me off."

"Well, what did you think was going to happen, Dolla?!" My mother looked at me like Jada had looked at me so many times; like I was a fucking idiot!

"I know I hurt her, ma, but dang. It hurt like a motherfucker to see her out with that nigga! She knew that shit was gon' hurt me!"

My mother laughed sarcastically. "You sound like a damn fool. You act like she did that on purpose-"

"She did!"

"How? Did she know you was gon' be there?"

"Nah."

"Exactly. But you knew what the fuck you were doing when you stuck your lil' dick-"

"My dick ain't little."

"Whateva, nigga!" she laughed. "You knew exactly what you were doing when you stuck your unprotected dick inside of that girl and made these babies. *That* was on purpose. You consciously hurt Jada over and over again. Now, after all these years, she finally says 'fuck you' and goes to get her some dick, and you got the audacity to be mad? At least she had the decency to wait until you alls relationship was over to do it. You are just hurt and jealous. And instead of telling her that, you gotta 'be a man' and act like you big mad." Then she sucked her teeth. "Shit, the least she coulda done was went out on a date. Hell, I'm proud of her."

I looked her upside her head. "Really, Ma?"

"Really," she smirked.

As I shook my head, she asked me, "What are you going to do, Dolla?"

"What you mean?"

"Do you want your family back?"

I frowned and waved my hand. "Not after she played me in front of everybody in that club!"

"Are you serious?"

"Hell yea."

My mother looked at me shamefully, but she didn't understand.

"Ma, it was not just seeing her with him. It was seeing how she treated me. She don't love me no more. She tired of me."

"You can fix that."

I dramatically looked at Bianca, then Brandon, and then back at my mother. "How? 'Cus I can't make them go away, and that's the only thing that will make Jada feel better."

My mother tapped my leg lightly, saying, "Trust me. If she rode with you through all that bullshit over the years, these babies won't make a bit of difference. Just give her some time...and some love."

Just as she said that, my phone started to ring again. All it took was a look from my mother for me to get it out of my pocket against my will. My mother leaned over, looked at the Caller ID and snatched the phone out of my hand.

"Ma, stop!" I told her. "I don't wanna talk to her."

"Shut up, boy! It's not her. It's her mother." Then she answered the phone, putting it on speaker phone. "Hey, Bev."

"Hey, Judy."

"What's going on, girl?' my mother asked her.

"Haaaave ...yooou... talked to Jada?"

The hesitation in Bev's voice made my mother suspicious, but it only pissed me off, making me wonder if Jada had the nerve to still be laid up with that nigga.

"No," my mother answered. "But she's called Dolla today."

Bev sounded relieved as she asked, "Oh good. Did they talk?"

Then my mother looked at me with a nasty smirk. "No. He missed her call."

"Can you please have him call her? She was supposed to pick up the kids this morning, but she didn't. I've been calling her all day, but she won't answer. I'm getting kind of worried. The kids are too."

"Okay. He'll call her, and we'll call you right back."

"Okay. Thanks."

My mother then hung up and started pushing other buttons. I knew that she was calling Jada, and I just let her so that she could hear how Jada's thot ass had been doing dicks all night and day, instead of picking up her fucking kids.

My mother still had the phone on speaker, so I heard that it took a few rings before the other line finally picked up. "You finally givin' your baby mama a callback, huh, nigga?"

I immediately snatched the phone from my mother as her eyes bucked.

"Who the fuck is this?!" I barked into the phone. "You bet' not be that nigga from last night! I'm fuckin' you up, nigga! Put Jada on the phone!"

Then, I heard Jada shrieking. "Dolla, heeeeelp!!"

My mom held her chest as I attempted to jump up but remembered that the baby was in my lap. My mother hurriedly laid lil' Brandon down on the couch and took Bianca from me. I finally jumped up and began to pace.

"SHUT UP, BITCH!" I heard him yell at Jada.

I could hear Jada cursing, "Fuck you!" I could even hear the tears in her eyes.

"Yea, nigga," he spoke into the phone. "You might wanna come help yo' bitch. Bring three-hundred thousand cash with you, or you can kiss this bitch goodbye. I'll call you back in an hour with a meetup spot."

Then he hung up.

CHAPTER SEVEN

KING

Saturday night, I woke up to a pounding sound on my front door. I jumped out of my sleep and didn't even bother to throw pants on over my boxers. Only the squad knew where I lived, and if one of them was pounding on my door like this, it was an emergency.

I flew down the stairs and towards the front door. Before snatching it open, I looked through the peephole and saw Meech and Dolla waiting impatiently.

I flung the door and immediately asked, "What's goin' on?"

They made their way into the foyer hurriedly.

"Man, joe, some dumb ass nigga don' kidnapped Jada."

I frowned towards Dolla and asked for clarification. "Kidnapped?"

I knew I had heard him right, but who the fuck still kidnapped people? This wasn't the fucking Taliban. This was the hood. People got shot or robbed; not fucking kidnapped. This had to be at the hands of a dumbass nigga.

"Last night she said she was going to have a drink with her cousins or some shit. What the fuck happened?" I asked.

Dolla sucked his teeth and shook his head with disgust. "Man, she was lying. She went out with some goofy ass nigga." As my eyes rolled the ceiling, he continued, "I went to check out LaMelle's Friday night and saw this bitch all hugged up with this big goofy ass lookin' motherfucka. So, I go right in there on dummy because I wasn't with the shits at all. I hem Jada up, she fighting me back and shit, and then Goofy step to me, so I go for my thang! Of course, the bouncers throw me out before I can air that bitch out. I texted the bitch all night; no reply. Then she starts blowing me up today, but I'm thinking, 'fuck that bitch.' But then her moms called looking for her all worried and shit. So I'm thinking, 'I know this bitch ain't laid up with this nigga.' So my mom calls her from my phone and this nigga answers, Jada screaming in the background, and he demandin' three-hundred thousand."

"What the fuck?!" I was blown!

"Exactly."

"You know this nigga or something?"

"Hell nah. And we know damn near everybody in the Chi. He gots to be some lame ass nigga if I don't know him, and he can't be in the Chi often."

"So how he know you got it like that? I know Jada ain't pillow talkin'."

"Exactly!"

"I don't see Jada pillow talkin'," Meech cut in. "She hurt and shit, so she clownin', but she ain't gon' go against us like that by talkin'. She wouldn't do that. She helped build this shit."

I nodded in agreement. That was real talk. Dolla was being too stubborn to see that shit, though.

"So what else he say?" I asked.

"He said he was gon' call me back in an hour with a drop spot. That was twenty minutes ago, but we on our way over there to blow our way through that bitch. Little do he or Jada know, it's a GPS on her truck. I just never had a reason to track that shit."

"So why didn't you go snatch her ass up when you was mad about her being with that nigga?" I asked.

Dolla snarled. "Because fuck that bitch. She wanna do dicks, then I'mma let her do dicks."

I held in my chuckle and just shook my head. This nigga was definitely in his feelings. Jada had hurt him...bad.

"Fuck you," he told me as he caught the look in my eyes. "The only reason I'm going to get the bitch now is because I love my kids, and I don't wanna see them hurt because I let some goofy ass nigga kill their mama over three hundred thousand. So let's go. I got the address where she is."

"How you know her car not somewhere else? She could have parked somewhere and hopped in the car with that nigga."

Dolla shrugged. "We 'bout to find out."

Relieved, I smiled, "Bet. Let me get dressed."

It had been a long time since I was in some action like this. We had lil' soldiers to take care of any of our problems. And even though we had killed Lock, that wasn't fun because I really didn't want to kill him. But this was about to be some old school shoot 'em up bang bang that I had given up a long time ago for the sake of maturity and staying out of jail. Jada was a good reason to go back to our old ways.

I ran upstairs wishing that I had had the time to put a GPS or even register the OnStar on Kennedy's Bentley. But we had left for the honeymoon as soon as I gave it to her and then the shit hit the fan not very long after we got back from Cabo. I never had the opportunity to do either. Now, I was kicking my ass for not making it a priority.

SIREN

"He finally called!"

I rolled my eyes at Marcus' eagerness. *Damn, this nigga is goofy.*

I rushed to close the bathroom door. Though Meech wasn't home, I didn't want to risk him coming back and hearing me.

"Okaaaay?" I asked and then paused, waiting for him to say something.

"I told him that I was going to call him back in an hour with a pickup location. We 'bout to get paid!"

I thought that before, but I highly doubted that Marcus could pull it off now. He had been way too sloppy, and he had no backup. I'd insisted that he get a friend to help, but he didn't want to split the money any further. I knew that there was no way that Dolla would show up alone. Yet, Marcus was a skilled thief. He jacked niggas for a living and had gotten away with it thus far, so I had a small amount of faith in him.

"You have to kill her." When I heard his hesitating breaths, I ensured him, "Look, you, don't be soft because you like that bitch. She knows your face. Once you get away with the money, Jada is going to tell them who you are. She knows a lot about you, and they got connections. It will be only a small amount of time before they catch up with your ass."

This was true, but I was also laying it on thick because I was trying to tie up loose ends. Jada knew my secrets, and now it was a possibility that I could be tied to this shit. That bitch had to go.

"Ah ight," he finally agreed softly.

"Cool. Tell them that you're going to meet them in a crowded place, like a restaurant or bar. That way they can't act all trigger-happy, and don't you get trigger-happy with them either. I want my money and my man. Don't shoot my nigga."

"Ah ight. Ah ight."

"Call me when you're done." Then a smile spread across my face. "And send me a pic of her body once you kill her."

"What?" he breathed in disbelief.

"I want to make sure you do it, nigga!"

"Fine. Whatever."

"*Call me back*," I urged.

"Okay."

I ended the call expecting to feel some sort of remorse, but I should have known better. Jada fucking deserved it. She had tried to kill me, shit! It was only fair.

Just as I was leaving out of the bathroom, my phone vibrated. It was Meech.

"Hello?"

"Hey. Elijah good?" From the urgency in his voice, I knew that he had found out about Jada.

"Yea, *we're* good. What's wrong?"

"I'll tell you later."

Then he hung up, and I giggled uncontrollably.

DOLLA

Jada should have known better than this. She had been fucking with a G', with a nigga that was famous in the Chi for being on. For those reasons alone, she shouldn't have had her goofy ass tramping around with some no-name nigga. Yea, I had my own reasons for not wanting her with another man, but on some business shit, she knew she had to be careful; she usually always was. The fact that she wasn't now let me know that the twins had her off her square. I felt bad, but, as we sat outside of the address where her car was, I still felt sick to my stomach. She was here to fuck that hurt away; I knew it. That's what hurt women did. Knowing that just left a fucked up taste in a nigga's mouth.

"That's her truck in the driveway. This gotta be that nigga's house."

This motherfucker had to be a goofy. He let her car sit right out front. That shit was sloppy as hell for a nigga who thought he was a criminal.

I knew everybody she knew; every family member, every female friend. We had been fucking damn near all of our lives. I knew everywhere she went, and this house was nowhere her people lived or nowhere she would usually be.

Meech pulled over a few houses down and killed the lights. It was almost time for the nigga to call me back, and I was getting anxious.

"We gotta go in now. That goofy motherfucka might kill her if he thinks we got that bread," I told King and Meech.

From the front seat, King and Meech both nodded.

"Call him and make sure that..." King hesitated. "...that he hasn't already..."

Visions of Meagan in that casket flashed before my eyes as I stared at the house, looking for any movement. I swallowed the lump in my throat and called Jada's phone with my phone on speaker so that King and Meech could hear what was going on.

I was starting to think that the nigga wouldn't answer once it rung four times, but eventually, he did. "I said I'd call you in an hour."

"I got your bread. Shit, I'm ready when you are."

"I'll call you back when it's been an hour, nigga."

"Well, let me hear her voice so I know she good."

The whack ass motherfucka sucked his teeth. I heard heavy footsteps like he was going up some stairs, so I stared at the house, hoping I would see something through the window that faced a set of stairs, and sure enough, I peeped that goofy ass nigga going up the stairs. But his figure disappeared as he ascended the stairs.

I heard a door open and close. Then I heard him barking at Jada, "Let this nigga know you okay."

There was some shuffling. Then Jada's voice was so close to the phone as if he was holding the phone to her ear. "Hello?" Her voice was so raspy and tired that I actually felt a lil' bad for her thot ass.

"You ah ight?" I spat.

"Yea." She had the nerve to be short with me! But that shit didn't last long. "What the fuck took you so long to answer my gawd damn calls, nig-"

King, Meech and I shook our heads in disbelief of Jada's persistent attitude.

Dumbass snapped, "Aye! Y'all ain't about to have no lovers' qu-qu..."

I closed my eyes in disbelief. "*Quarrel*. Lovers' quarrel, motherfucka!"

King and Meech laughed a little.

"Aye, fuck you, nigga!" Dumbass snapped. "You heard she ah ight. I'll call you back when I have a location."

Then he hung up. Again, I fought to see through the darkness and through the window. As I did, I saw him coming back down the stairs.

"We gotta go now," I told them.

"Let's go."

We all put our hoods over our heads before getting out of my trap car and running through the Saturday night, summertime air on the suburban block in Bellwood. It was a nice quiet block, so, though it was a Saturday night, nobody was outside to see three men dressed in dark clothing and hoods running towards a house with guns gripped tightly in their hands.

Getting into the crib wasn't hard at all. Like I said, this nigga had to be a goofy. He had no one on lookout or security. King used his powerful legs to kick down the door.

Dumbass was jumping up off of the couch as we barged through. He immediately started to run towards the back of the house, but I caught up with his goofy ass in the hallway and smashed his ass in the back of the head with my gun.

"Where the fuck you runnin', bitch?" I threatened as he buckled to his knees. King was behind me because he had accompanied me in chasing this dumb motherfucker. I could hear heavy footsteps heading up the stairs, so I knew Meech was going to check up on Jada.

Then I heard Meech yell, "Get the keys to the cuffs before you kill that nigga!"

King had his gun pointed at the goofy nigga's dome as I snatched his ass up to his feet.

"Where the keys at, nigga?" I spat.

"Fuck y'all!" Even though this nigga was an obvious goofy, he was trying to save face. So, I let one off in his leg to show his ass I wasn't playin'.

The sound of the shot couldn't be heard because I had a silencer on my shit; we all did.

"Aaargh!" he cringed like a bitch. He clutched his legs as I held his shirt so tight by the collar that it had to be choking him.

"Give me the fuckin' keys, nigga! I don't feel like playin' with y-" Then I just got fed the fuck up. "You know what? Fuck this!" Then I put two right into his temple.

"Nigga, how we gon' get her out now?" King asked as the goofy's body slumped down on the dark hardwood floors.

I shrugged, not giving a fuck at this point. This lame ass nigga was getting on my nerves. Jada was getting on my nerves. I didn't give a fuck about shit.

King bent down over this fool's dying body. He reached right past his brains leaking out of his head, into his jean pockets and pulled out a set of keys.

"These looks like they may be it," he said as he held two small keys that were on the key ring.

"Fine," I said as I headed towards the stairs with King on my tail.

As we climbed the steps, I noticed that Meech was standing outside the room with a weird look on her face.

"Why are you standing out here?" King asked.

"She… Uhhh… She naked, bruh."

Meech and King stood looking at me with fucked up looks on their faces, waiting for my response to my bitch being naked in another man's bed, meaning the he had obviously fucked her by will or force.

As I climbed the last few steps, I wished that that nigga was alive just so that I could kill his ass again.

"Let me go secure the door and make sure nobody heard shit," Meech said as he walked down the stairs past us.

King went with him. "I'll help you, bruh."

Fuck them. Them niggas just didn't want to be there when this shit hit the fan. They knew that this shit was fucking with me and not because Jada had been kidnapped by some clown. They knew that this shit was fucking with me because she was with this nigga in the first place!

Chapter Eight

DOLLA

As soon as I opened the door, I saw Jada's naked ass just laying on the bed on her back looking straight up at the ceiling. She was bound by her wrists and ankles by handcuffs. She had the nerve not to even look me in my fucking face. I hoped her silly ass was embarrassed. She looked beat the fuck up. Her brown skin was red and purple on her face. Clumps of some shit I couldn't recognize, but stunk like a motherfucker, was in her hair. I just quietly unlocked the cuffs as I heard chainsaws starting downstairs. Meech and King were most likely cleaning up that lame nigga's body.

After she was completely free of the cuffs, Jada tried to get up, but she was struggling like a motherfucker.

I went to grab her arm to help her, and she violently swatted my hand away, screeching, "I don't need your motherfucking help!"

"Fuck you too then!"

"No, fuck you, Dolla! I been getting my ass whooped for damn near two days because of you! I been calling your ass all day! You so mad that you was willing to let me die?! Fuck you!"

I probably should have felt some sympathy for the tears in her eyes, but fuck that. The fact remained the same. This nigga wouldn't have had the opportunity to pull this whack ass move if she wasn't in here pussy poppin'!

When I chuckled, it only pissed her off even more. "Shiiiid, it wasn't because of me! It was because of your thot ass!"

"Thot?!"

"Didn't nobody tell yo' ass to go tryin' to fuck some nigga 'cus you mad!"

Then she had the nerve to try to lie. "I didn't fuck him!"

Instantly, I bent down and reached for the used condom that I had seen by the bed when I was unlocking the handcuffs. I threw it at her, and it hit her right in the fucking nose. "You didn't fuck him?! Then what's that?!"

The condom landed in her lap, and she swatted it away with embarrassment. I reached for her clothes on the dresser and started to throw them at her. As the bra hit her in the face, I wished that that shit felt like a brick hitting her in her dome.

"STOP!" she shouted as she tried to catch everything that I threw at her.

I was launching everything at her; shorts, top, panties, shoes.

"Would you stop?!" she shouted, as she tried to catch it all, too weak to fight me back like her eyes showed she really wanted to.

King then walked into the room, and when he saw that Jada was still naked, he stopped at the doorway and turned his back. "Aye, y'all gotta cool out until we get out of here. Y'all can't be attracting attention with all that screaming."

"Then come get your friend," Jada sneered.

"No," I interjected. "Come get your thot ass friend, King."

"Dolla," King said with a warning tone, still with his back turned. "Cool out. She been through enough."

"She wouldn't have been through shit if she wasn't being a hoe."

We shot each other menacing, threatening stares as King said, "C'mon now-"

"Nah, she a hoe. She fucked this nigga. The condom still on the floor."

Without even knowing what he was doing, he turned his head, saw the condom on the floor and looked at Jada with a shameful look. Then he remembered that she was naked and turned his head.

"Aye, fuck you, King!" Jada spat as she finished getting dressed. "Don't fucking look at me like that! Both you niggas got kids outside of your relationship that your bitches didn't know about. Y'all ain't shit! Ain't neither one of you niggas innocent, so fuck you, Dolla, and fuck you, King! How long you expect your bitch to put up with your bullshit before she show you how if feel?! Huh?! How long y'all expect to play loyal bitches with bum bitches and expect that loyal bitch to still be there? Loyal means unconditionally loving you, not loving you while you continue to hurt us until you KILL US with the pain you're inflicting on us!" She threw her leg into her shorts as she continued to rant and rave while staring into my eyes with tears streaming down her tired eyes. "How long did you expect me to keep sleeping next to you but feeling alone?! Knowing that it was another bitch out here getting the attention that I earned while I was being some loyal, ride or die bitch to you?! FUCK Y'ALL!"

She flung her arms through her halter and struggled to stand on her feet. I wanted to help her. I wanted to tell her she was right. But I was too ornery to do either, so I just continued to glare at her with a threatening stare.

She snatched up her purse and then walked towards King, asking, "Where the fuck is my phone?!"

King stuttered. "I-I don't know."

If I tried to act like I wasn't fazed by her words, King couldn't help but show his empathy. I knew it was because he was weak over the shit that he was putting Kennedy through.

"Marcus had it!" Jada fussed. "Get my shit before you bury that nigga!"

She didn't wait for a response. She pushed past King and struggled to go down the stairs.

King looked back at me with a judgmental stare. "Help her, nigga."

But I was still being an asshole. "Man, fuck her."

King shook his head and hurried after Jada, and I reluctantly followed.

JADA

"I don't need your fucking help, King!" I barked as I swatted his helping hand away.

"Jada, chill out. You look hurt. Let me help you."

Because of the sincerity in King's voice, I broke down in tears as I gripped the rail. "He should be helping me!"

"Well, he ain't. I am. So c'mon." He took my arm into his as he asked, "You okay? You need to go to the hospital?"

"No," I cried. "I just want to take a bath, and I want some sleep."

As I heard Dolla's footsteps close behind, I sucked up my tears. Fuck that, I wasn't going to let that nigga see me cry or being weak, so I quickly wiped my face.

Fuck that bitch. He had a lot of nerve. Yes, maybe fucking another nigga so soon was a bit much, but those gawd damn twins was a bit much. *His* thot ass had been spreading his dick all over town, but he wanted to look at me like I was the hoe for finally treating him like he had been treating me.

Fuck him!

As I finally got to the bottom of the stairs and turned the corner, I saw Meech hovering over a mound of bloody flesh that he was about to wrap in plastic.

"Wait! My phone is in his pocket!"

I went towards Meech, but I was so weak and fatigued from hunger and the beatings that I wasn't moving fast, and I was limping.

"I got it," King said stopping me. I could see Dolla out of my peripheral standing behind me, with his ornery ass.

I watched as King bent over the remains of Marcus' body. After a few seconds, he came towards me with my phone in his hand. "You need to leave. Go get some rest. We gotta get this shit cleaned up."

My eyes bucked, and I folded my arms. "Leave with who?!" When King hesitated, I knew what he was about to say, so I stopped him. "I'm not going with him. I'll drive my truck."

"You shouldn't be driving."

He was right. I was too weak to even climb into the truck, and if I managed that, I was liable to fall asleep driving. "Why can't you take me home?"

"Dolla drove. One of the guys is on his way so that we can go dump this body. Plus, I found that nigga's phone. I need to put somebody on tracing his calls to see who else was in on this shit." I still wasn't budging, so he started to beg. "C'mon, Jada. Please? We don't have time for this shit. We gotta move. I'll make sure your truck gets to the crib."

It pissed me off that King was being more caring and kind to me than my own damn babies' daddy. King wasn't the one that deserved my stubbornness or anger, so I just turned and marched out of the door. As the fresh air hit my face, I was happy as hell that I was alive but disappointed about it at the same time. It would have been so much better if I was unable to feel this hurt anymore. But I quickly remembered my children, who were probably worried like crazy about me. I had to shake this shit so that I could be a better parent to them than their ratchet ass father. I couldn't keep making dumb ass decisions, like being vulnerable to some goofy ass nigga, just for the sake of getting dick.

I leaned against Dolla's trap car. Dolla slowly walked towards the car like he didn't give a fuck about shit. He didn't even open the passenger side door for me. He just popped the lock and got in on his side. Swear to God, if I had the strength, I would have fucking walked home, but I wasn't about to give Dolla the benefit of getting rid of me. I knew he was just coming at my head because he was hurt that, after all these years of being by his side no matter what he did, I had stepped out on him. He had to sit with the visual of some nigga's dick in me, just as I had to sit with my fucked up visuals.

That's what he get!

I had no fucking remorse as I climbed into the car and slammed the door.

We rode in complete silence. He didn't ask me if I okay, how I felt...nothing. He sat his ornery ass over there like I was the one that did something to him.

♪ Heavy
What you know about a young rich nigga gettin' money
Everybody call him heavy
What you know about a young rich nigga spend 1700 on a set
I gotta new foreign coupe back then
I ain't had a box Chevy
fuck nigga now I'm heavy
I used to be broke now, I'm heavy♪

He was bumping Blac Youngsta at an ignorant volume. I knew he was doing it just to piss me off, so I lay back in the seat, staring out of the window, appearing unbothered on the outside, but fuming on the inside all the way back to King's crib.

Once we arrived and Dolla turned into the circular driveway, Dolla remained silent. My body ached as I collected my things. We both stayed quiet and avoided one another's eyes, as I opened the door. He didn't even bother to help me or to open the door for me. Even after the danger I'd faced for the past two days, the bitch didn't even bother to offer to walk me inside to ensure my safety. I slammed the car door, fighting back tears, still refusing to show him any further weakness. Even as I walked towards the front door, he was pulling out of the driveway before I could even get my key out.

That's when I broke down. As I opened King's front door, I cried hysterically, harder than I did as I lay in Marcus' bed, naked, cold and waiting to die. As I secured the door behind myself, I knew that I had to get my shit together. I wanted my mother to bring me my kids so that I could lie in bed with them watching movies, after taking a long, hot, steaming bath. I couldn't do that if I was crying like this, not after the way that I had been acting in front of them lately. The embarrassment of the realization that I had been so mad that I subjected my kids to this craziness made the tears flow even stronger. That, on top of the embarrassment of Marcus making a further fool out of me, in front of the other nigga that had made a complete fool out of me, made me buckle to my knees. But I had to get it together. I knew that I had to change so that I could be a mother to my kids, so that Brittany never experienced this, and so that Brandon never hurt a woman in this way. I also knew that, if it wasn't clear before, as I leaned against the stone wall in King's foyer, crying unbelievably, I knew then that me and Dolla were definitely over.

CHAPTER NINE

KENNEDY

♪ *Every since you went away*
I ain't been doing nothing but
(Thinking, thinking, thinking, thinking
With my head in my hands
Thinking

You been away for so long
And I just don't think I can carry on so I start
(Drinking, drinking drinking drinking
Each and every night
(Drinking) ♪

As I stepped out of the shower, I heard music that made me think of my mother and father, who I had finally talked to after getting a cell phone. They had a million questions, especially since I had called them anonymous. Of course, they assumed that I was into some shit that would land me back in prison. But after telling them that me and King were into it and that I was leaving him, they understood.

I think my father was also elated!

Since it was after midnight, I wondered what Glen could be doing, so I threw on a robe and followed the sultry music. Once in the den, I saw him sitting and clutching a glass of a brown liquid.

I laughed, only because, on the outside, he looked like I felt on the inside. We were both still mourning the loss of Ms. Jerry, but the pain on his face, the pain in my heart, that I masked during the day in order to be a mother to Kayla, was far beyond being sad that Ms. Jerry was gone.

Our hearts were broken.

When I giggled, he jumped a bit and looked back at me. Once looking into my eyes, he didn't bother to mask his pain.

"Listening to this shit isn't going to make you feel any better," I joked as I slid into the room.

When Glen chuckled in response, I sat on the couch beside him. "What's this anyway?" I asked.

Glen looked at me like I was crazy, just like he did every time I asked him which artist he was listening to when he blasted this old skool shit. Though Glen was in his mid-twenties, he listened to the same old artists that I heard my parents blasting when I was little. I never liked it very much, but as Glen's parents blasted it, he loved it and caught an addiction to it.

"That's Teddy Pendergrass."

I frowned, asking, "Who?"

He rolled his eyes and shook his head as if he couldn't believe my ignorance. "He's the shit."

"He's depressing."

"He's not depressing. He misses his woman. Don't he sound like he miss her?"

I shut my judgmental lips long enough to listen.

♪ 'Cause I (Oh, I) Oh, I (Oh, I)

(Miss you) I miss you, baby

(Miss you)

(Miss you, miss you)

Oh, Lord (Miss you)

You can look at my eyes and see

That a great big man like me has been

(Crying, crying) [2x]

Crying my heart and soul out to you, baby

(Crying)

Sitting in my lonely room

Filled with nothing but gloom and I feel like

(Dying, dying) [2x]

Hey, y'all help me

(Dying) ♪

King was always on my mind, but those lyrics and the passion in that man's voice really had him on my mind then, but I quickly shook it off. I was tired of constantly talking about King to Glen, so I fought the urge and asked him, "Do you miss her?"

Glen didn't think twice before snarling and shaking his head.

He spat, "Hell no," and then took another shot of Hennessy.

I reached towards the stack of plastic red cups for one and aimed it towards him.

He poured me a cup of Hennessy with no chaser as he asked me, "You miss him?"

"I'm too pissed to miss him." When Glen didn't reply, only continued to stare at the black screen of the television, I asked, "Is that fucked up?"

He quickly shook his head. "Hell nah. What he did was fucked up, yo'; especially after all you did for him. You're a good woman…" He paused and looked at me. I saw the intoxication in his eyes as his eyes left mine and traveled down my body; something he usually attempted to do discreetly, but the Hennessy had him feeling froggish, I guess. And I guess hurt had me feeling froggish because I didn't hide from his eyes, nor did I bother to cover the parts of my body that were being slightly exposed by the robe I'd slipped on. "You're a badass woman. You're down as fuck. King is stupid as shit for hurting you."

Every word he said was spoken to my thighs. His eyes never moved from my curves until I took a long, big shot of Hennessey. Maybe it was the pregnancy hormones, but his words had my pussy leaking. In my twenty-one years, I had only been around two men that I was attracted to so much that I wanted to fuck them, wanted to sit on their face. Unfortunately... Glen was the third. For the past few days, I had been attempting to ignore my attraction to him and the way he respectfully, yet discreetly, checked me out. I figured that I was just hurting after what King did and was looking to make it feel better anyway that I could. But, shit, I was sober as I sat there and still wanted to just have Glen on top of me for a lil' while, something that reminded me of the love I used to feel.

I tried to keep it together though. I let Glen continue to talk about how much of the shit I was as I sipped the Hennessy and hoped that the throbbing, pulsating pounding in my pussy would go away. I fought the urge to check out the bulge that was sitting comfortably on his thigh as he spoke highly of me for thirty minutes.

Damn, it's not even hard.

I hadn't been with another man in so long. I had been so stupidly loyal to King because he had made me feel like he was just as loyal to me. But as the liquor started to take effect, I cursed myself for missing out on so much because I was loyal to a nigga that wasn't being a smidge as loyal to me.

Fuck this.

I needed it. I needed to be held, touched, something, anything. I needed arms around me, squeezing this pain until it went away, if only for a moment. And this nigga was too respectful to take this pussy, so I went for it. It reminded me of when I had done this the first time that I met King. I had given him my body because I was heartbroken then, and I was hurt now. As I climbed towards Glen, who looked at me with wide, curious eyes, I wondered if this sex would lead to all that the sex with King had.

The reluctance in Glen's eyes made me feel like he would stop me at any moment; however, as I straddled him and put my lips on top of his, he didn't. As I sucked his tongue, it surprised me how sweet and good his mouth tasted. Then his hand raced under my robe and grabbed my ass. I was surprised at the moan that escaped my lips so easily. It felt so good to have strong arms wrapped around me and rough hands on my skin. But it was also so new because it wasn't King. Yet, being in the arms of someone besides King was something that I would have to start getting used to.

When I felt Glen pulling his mouth from mine, I opened my eyes and saw the reluctance in his.

"What's wrong?" I asked.

He sighed deeply. I felt his huge erection as I sat on his lap watching his eyes avoid mine as he told me, "You shouldn't do this."

"Why not?"

When he answered, "You love him," I felt silly and slid off his lap and onto the couch next to him. "Don't do this because you're hurting. Don't hurt him because he hurt you."

I pouted. My lip was literally poking out as I folded my arms.

"C'mon now, Kennedy. Don't be like that. You know I'd fuck the shit out of you. I like you, ma, but we shouldn't go there if you're still in love with King."

"I'm n-"

"You still love that nigga. Don't deny it."

Fuck him for being such a damn gentlemen, I thought.

I could feel Glen's eyes on me. When I looked at him, he had the nerve to be smiling at me, and he looked fucking gorgeous.

"You know I'm right," he said, nudging me.

"Whatever," I mumbled.

"You need to call him. It's been like a week."

"I don't have shit to say to him."

"Then let him talk to Kayla. He's probably worried."

I huffed as I stood to my feet. The room spun a little bit, and that's when I knew I was tipsy. "Good night, Glen."

"Don't ignore me," I heard him say.

"*Good night.*"

I heard him chuckle as I walked out.

Forget him. I was trying to have dirty, drunk sex, and he wanted to talk about King.

Urgh!

SIREN

"Mom!"

I stopped walking and made an about-face when I heard Elijah calling for me from the den. I peeked my head in and saw him and Meech sitting on the couch and Transformers playing on the flat screen.

"Yes, baby?"

"Come watch the movie with us. It just started."

"Yea, c'mon," Meech insisted.

My heart smiled. Meech was still being nice to me but we still weren't officially back together, so every time he did anything that still resembled us being a family, I was geeked and felt like I was closer to getting my man back.

I abandoned the idea of washing, which I was on my way to do before Elijah stopped me. I walked into the den and Elijah made room for me to sit next to his dad. When I sat, Meech actually put his arm around me, and I almost fainted. Clearly, I had put Jada through all of that shit for no reason. It was looking like I didn't need the money to leave at all. When Meech came home and told me what happened, I was relieved that Marcus was killed before he could tell them that I had anything to do with it. Lucky for me, they were so busy slanging guns that they hadn't asked any questions or gone through his phone. Unfortunately, for me, Jada was still alive with my secrets to tell.

JADA

"What the fuck do you want? The kids are downstairs. You came to see them, right?"

I rolled my eyes hard as hell before returning my eyes to the TV in the guest bedroom. I hadn't left that bed since I got there the night before. Besides being sore and worn out, my heart hurt so bad that I didn't have the strength to leave the bed. I lied to the kids, telling them that I had the flu, so they wouldn't bother me. King had been so attentive to them all day. He felt horrible about what happened to me and was as sympathetic as Dolla should have been. Dolla hadn't texted or called me. The only reason he was there now was because the kids wanted to see him. Brandon missed him terribly. I was starting to look like the Cruella Deville to them because I was keeping their father from them, so I finally gave in.

"I gotta talk to you."

I sucked my teeth, huffed and puffed so damn dramatically that I know I looked petty as hell. But I didn't want to talk to that nigga. I didn't want to be in his presence. Every pain that I was feeling at that moment was because of him. Even what Marcus had done to me was Dolla's fault, because had he not hurt me, I would have been home instead of somewhere with that nigga with my ass in the air like a goof ball.

"For real. I need your help."

I looked at that motherfucker like he was crazy. "Help? Fuck you."

"Fuck our kids, though? Because if we don't get rid of this detective bitch and Siren, the squad gon' end up in jail and ain't nobody gon' be out here to take care of them."

I cringed because the nigga was right, and I hated that shit. This motherfucker didn't even deserve my motherfucking eye contact, let alone my help. But shit, on the inside, behind the anger in my heart, I knew that, after seeing that rubber, Dolla was just as hurt as me, so he was probably only asking for my help because he absolutely had to. But I hated the fact that he had the nerve to be standing in the doorway looking at me as if I was the one that wasn't shit. A nigga can fuck every bitch in the world, your friends, the random ratchet bitch at the bar, your damn sister, and you take him back every time. However, let you fuck one nigga that he can't even point out in a crowd and this nigga is devastated! He done fucked several bitches on me, but I fucked one and this nigga look like he wanna die. The nerve!

I was taking too long to respond, so Dolla tried to further persuade me. He sighed heavily as he looked me right in the eyes. "King stopped me on my way up the stairs. He said he just got a call back on that trace on your goof ball's cell phone..."

"Your goof ball." I hate this nigga, I thought as my eyes rolled.

Dolla ignored my attitude and continued, "They found calls and text messages between him and his 'partner.'... It was Siren."

My eyes bulged. I quickly sat up and felt pain in every part of my upper body. "WHO?"

"This is why I need your help-"

"That bitch!" I spat as I ran my hand over my head. "I'm killing that bitch!"

I couldn't believe it! This bitch, Siren, was a fucking psychopath! This bitch had to be certified fucking crazy! There was no limits to this bitch's deceit. She had to die!... For real this time!

"You can't do anything," Dolla insisted. "We're taking care of it, and it has to be done a certain way."

I glared at Dolla. I couldn't believe this shit. Fuck Siren and fuck Dolla! The two of them were the loves of my lives, and now I wanted nothing more than to attend their fucking funerals!

"Jada, I'm serious. We're taking care of this shit, but I really need your help. If you don't want to do it for the kids, do it because you deserve to make this bitch pay."

Urgh! "What is that you need me to do?"

CHAPTER TEN

SIREN

Monday morning, I was doing the laundry that I never finished the day before because I was watching the movie with Meech and Elijah. As I sat on the bed in my room folding the towels, a smile spread across my face thinking about the time we all spent together the night before as a family. After Transformers had gone off, Meech suggested that we watch another. He even ordered pizza. It felt like old times, minus us ending the night with him inside of me, but I knew the time was coming soon.

"Siren!"

I was shocked to see Jada in the doorway. Her eyes were big as shit, and her breathing was heavy as she stormed in. I thought for a second that the anger in her eyes was because she found out that I was behind her kidnapping, until she said, "I thought you said you weren't talking to that detective bitch anymore?"

She was so loud that I feared Meech would hear. He was downstairs in the den watching TV, but I still rushed towards the bedroom door and shut it. "I haven't talked to her."

"Well, she showed up at my house questioning Dolla again, and she mentioned Meech too. She said she got the evidence that she needs to arrest all three of them."

My heart started to beat out of my chest. Jada huffed and puffed as she washed her hands over her face.

"What the fuck are we gonna to do, Siren?" she asked me. "If they go to jail, we popped! What the fuck does she know? What did you tell her?"

"Nothing! I swear."

"You lyin'!"

"I promise!"

"How am I supposed to believe you? You talked to the bitch before and one of us ended up in jail!"

Before I could say anything, Jada's eyes narrowed at me like I was the most disloyal bitch in the world. To her, I was sure I was. Then she stormed past me, but the bitch looked so mad that I was scared to stop her, for fear that she would start so much drama that Meech would hear us.

Instead of stopping her, I got my phone out of my pocket and texted Maria.

Me: *I need to meet up with you.*

I started putting on my clothes because I planned on meeting up with Maria as soon as she hit me back. This bitch had me fucked up. She needed to lay off. Getting rid of King was one thing, and I didn't give a fuck about that at first. But Meech? That nigga was a no-no. Not my nigga. Not the father of my child.

By the time that I had thrown on a pair of skinny jeans, tube top, and sandals, my text message notification was chiming. I rushed towards the phone and was relieved when I saw that it was a message from Maria.

Maria: *I'd love to. Where?*

I shot her a text message, telling her to meet me in the Walmart parking lot that was about twenty minutes away. Then I grabbed my purse and keys and rushed downstairs.

"Meech! Meech, I'll be back!" I didn't even bother to go towards the den. I went straight for the front door.

"Where you goin'?" I heard him ask.

"Jewel's. I need some shrimp for dinner tonight."

He thought nothing of it. "Okay. Elijah goin' with you?"

"No. He's still in the backyard playing. Check on him in a few minutes."

"Okay."

I rushed out and into the garage. I thought of Meech getting arrested as my eyes fell on my Porsche. If the guys got arrested, we were going to lose all of this; Jada wouldn't even trust me enough to move dope with me in their absence, and Kennedy wasn't 'bout that life whatsoever. I had come too close to losing everything recently. Now, here I was again, with a normal life at my fingertips and yet again, someone or something was threatening to take that shit away from me.

I raced to the Jewel first, to pick up some shrimp so that I wouldn't look suspect when I got back home. Then I hurried to the Walmart. On my way, I tried to think of ways to get rid of Maria myself. She, along with Jada, was a thorn in my side. Those two women could fuck up everything for me, and I could not let that happen.

****

Twenty minutes later, I spotted Maria's Jeep Cherokee in the back of the Walmart parking lot. She got out as I was flying into the parking spot next to her. It was a hot, July day, and this was one of the times that I rarely saw Maria in casual clothes. In a tube top dress and heels, Maria actually looked pretty. I didn't give a fuck how pretty she looked, though. This bitch was about to get an ugly ass whooping fuckin' with mine.

"What the fuck is going on?" I spat as I marched towards her.

Maria looked at me strangely, but before she could even say anything, screeching tires caught our attention. A blacked out Chevy was racing through the parking lot in our lane. I thought it was some crazy kids until the window rolled down as the Chevy approached me and Maria. Being a detective, Maria's instincts were on high. My anger no longer had her attention. She reached into her purse just as shots came from the Chevy!

Pow! Pow! Pow!

"Arrgh!" I screamed as I hit the ground.

Pow! Pow! Pow!

I could hear glass shattering around me as the screams of others pierced the air!

Pow! Pow! Pow! Pow!

It seemed like the shooting would never stop. But then it did. Suddenly everything went silent. All I heard was the Chevy peeling off.

Then I heard Maria's irritating accent. "Bitch, you set me up!"

I jumped to my feet, surprised that Maria or I hadn't been hit. "No, I d-"

"Do you know the fucking time you can get for killing a fucking cop, you dumb bitch?!"

"I didn't do shit! I swear!"

"Did King know you were coming here?" As I shook my head with eyes full of confusion, she continued to hit me with questions. "What about Meech? Did he know? Dolla? Anybody?"

"No," I told her, But I still wondered what if one of them was on to me. I wondered if Jada's weak ass had said something and now they were trying to get rid of me and Maria. The fucked up thing was, I couldn't say shit to any one of them in order to find out without giving myself up.

"Shit, who knew *you* were here?" I asked Maria. "King the only nigga you stalkin'?"

That shit didn't work. Maria was pissed. She snatched her car door open, burning a hole into my face with her eyes. In the distance, police sirens could be heard.

"Get the fuck out of here and don't call me ever again," she said as she jumped into the car.

Fuck! I thought as she sped off.

Since the sounds of sirens were coming louder and closer, I was forced to shake off the uneasy feeling and rushed towards my Porsche. As I jumped in and turned the engine, all kinds of thoughts rushed through my head. I wondered if Jada had run her fucking mouth and told the crew about me talking to Maria. But considering that I was still living in Meech's house and he was being so nice, I didn't think that was the case at all. For all I knew, Jada's trigger-happy ass could have been the one trying to get rid of me and Maria. Shit, Maria's corrupt-cop-ass could be into some dirty shit her damn self.

I made the twenty-minute drive back home running every possibility through my mind. But as I turned into our driveway and hit the remote for the garage, I was still as lost as I was in that Walmart parking lot. Just as soon as things were looking good, they were turning bad again just that fast. It was crazy how I was willing to lose Meech a few weeks ago, and now I realized more than ever exactly how much he meant to me. I needed him more than anything and could not afford to lose him to anyone; not London, not Maria...Nobody.

"What's wrong with you?"

Meech's voice shocked the shit out of me as I locked the door. I jumped out of my skin but quickly tried to recover. But it was too late; he saw the fear and anxiety in my eyes.

"You okay?"

"Yea," I lied, as I started to dance a bit. "I just have to pee. I'm about to piss on myself."

I tossed him the Jewel's bag with the shrimp in it. Then I ran past him and his curious eyes and up the stairs. I wanted so badly to confess everything to him so that he could do what he had to do to ensure that he stayed out here getting money, but the truth would only have me at the fucking homeless shelter.

I would have to figure this shit out on my own.

LONDON

"Oh...my...God."

Initially, I had rushed out of my mom's crib in a hurry to get to the bus stop. I was on my way to work, and I was late. But the sight in the driveway had made me completely stuck.

"Oh my God," left my lips in a whisper as I inched closer to the white, 2016, Infinity truck parked in my mother's driveway with a huge, red bow placed on top of it.

I reached into my purse for my phone and quickly dialed my best friend in Michigan. Since the first day that I met Meech, I had been talking Twanya's ear off about him. Then, when that bitch showed up at the hotel that day, I had been crying on the phone with Twanya everyday about him.

Man, that nigga broke my heart. Mind you, I wasn't in love with him or nothing. We had just met. But his fine, down-to-earth, rich nigga ass was a fucking breath of fresh air. I didn't think it was men out here still like him. I was totally convinced that he was putting on a front; that the sweet, attentive man with an awesome dick that actually liked me had to be a fraud. And I was right! This nigga had a bitch living in his crib the whole time!

Urgh!

My heart and my pussy were broken.

"Hello?"

"Twanya! You ain't gon' believe this shit!"

"What?"

"There is a fucking 2016 Infinity truck in my mother's driveway with a fucking bow on it!"

She gasped. "Oooo! What kind?!"

"A QX80," I answered.

Twanya started to giggle, and I growled with irritation because we both knew who was behind this.

"I hate him!" I whined.

"Hate him? He bought you a truck with your walking, taking-public-transportation-ass. And he didn't only buy you any truck; he bought you a *seventy-thousand dollar truck*. You need to be grateful. Call him and tell him thank you...and then give him some pussy... a lot of it... and suck his dick... and you better swallow, bitch."

"See? That's exactly why I don't want this fucking truck. He's trying to buy my cooperation."

"Cooperation?"

"Yes, cooperation."

"Cooperation with what?"

"Cooperation with being his side bitch!"

Twanya sucked her teeth. "But I thought he said they were broken up."

"The bitch still live there, so..." My head began to hurt as I stared at the truck. The eighty-degree sun shined down on it, making it shine like a diamond. My bum ass hadn't had a man that ever splurged on me. Me and my ex lived together back in Michigan, but shit, we were going half on the bills, and nine times out of ten, he was late on his half, so I had to pay it to keep the utilities on. So, when Meech bought me a cell phone, I was floored! You would have thought the nigga proposed! And now a truck? A *new* truck? A bitch was moved...completely. But a truck wasn't going to change the fact that he came with baggage! Everybody has baggage, I know. But shit, his baggage wanted to fight and cut bitches in the face!

Ain't nobody got time for that!

"Let me call you back, Twanya."

I hung up without even waiting for her to say goodbye. I had deleted Meech's contact information from my phone and blocked any calls and text messages from his number. But, in the short time that I'd known him, I'd memorized the number any damn way. I was marching around the truck with my hands on my hips waiting for him to answer.

Damn, it even has rims.

"Hel-"

"Come get this shit!" When he laughed, it pissed me off even more. "This shit ain't funny! Come get this fucking truck, Meech!"

"Why?"

"Because I can't be bought!"

"I'm not trying to buy you. You deserve it. No strings attached."

I don't know whether it was the sound of his voice that was making me completely weak in the knees, or if it was his sincerity that was overwhelming me, but I was stuck, with no words to say.

"For real, ma. I told you, we didn't know each other for that long, but I was feeling you. Just because you refuse to talk to me, don't mean a nigga stopped caring about you. And I can't have nobody I care about on the bus. So just take it. The keys are in the ignition; just open the door. Okay?"

I hesitantly reached for the driver's side door, and it really did open. I peeked into the truck and sure enough, the keys were in the ignition. "O...okay..."

I wanted to say something else. I wanted to thank him and still curse him out for hurting me, but he quickly said, "Cool. Bye." Then he just hung up.

Motherfucka!

KING

Something told me to go back to Dre's house to see if she'd talked to Kennedy. Ever since the day that I burst into Dre's mother's house, I knew that she wouldn't really contact me if she heard from Kennedy. The two of them were too close, and if Kennedy didn't want her to, she wouldn't. But I was willing to do what I had to do to get the information out of her that I needed that night. It had been over a week, and I hadn't seen or heard from my queen or my princess. Shit, the distance wasn't this great when she was in prison. A nigga was starting to lose it.

Just as I pulled up on Dre's block, I saw her leaving out of the crib and jumping into the car. Something told me to just follow Dre, so I did. I stayed about three cars behind her as I followed her for about twenty minutes to this crib in Beverly. I noticed that the crib was nice as fuck as I parked a few houses down. Then I peeped Kennedy's Bentley truck in the driveway and lost it! I mean, a nigga was relieved, but then I got pissed off just that quick as I peeped the bikes in the driveway. Those motorcycles belonged to a nigga, which meant this house belonged to a nigga! And if Kennedy had been laid up with a nigga all this time, I was killing him, and it was going to take everything in me not to kill her.

My phone rang, snapping me out of my murderous trance.

"Yo," I answered without even looking to see who it was.

"Yea, bruh. That shit worked. Meech say Siren at home spooked like a motherfucka. I know it wasn't part of the plan, but I wish those bullets could have hit them bitches." Then he laughed. I would have found some humor in the shit too if I wasn't watching some nigga walk out of the house that I saw Dre go into with my daughter's hand in his.

I washed my hands over my face in attempt to keep myself from jumping out of my car and lighting this whole block up. My eyes squinted, trying to watch what this lame ass nigga was doing with Kayla. He'd disappeared into the garage with her and they emerged a few seconds later. She was in a pink, Camaro Power Wheel, and dude was behind her, protecting her, as she rode up and down the driveway.

"Yo'? Bruh?" I heard Dolla calling.

"Yea, I'm here."

"What the fuck is wrong with you?"

"I found Kennedy."

"Word? Where?"

"Some nigga house. I ain't went in yet."

Soon as I said that shit, Dolla was on it. "Where you at, bro? I'm on my way."

"Some house in Beverly. I'm 'bout to shoot you the address."

CHAPTER ELEVEN

KING

Dolla showed up with Meech not even an hour later, but we sat outside that crib until a little after midnight; long enough to watch the dude finish playing with Kayla in the driveway and to watch Dre leave about three hours later.

I thought it was best that we caught everybody in the house off guard when we burst through that motherfucker. I didn't know who this nigga was, so in case he was some trigger happy nigga, I wanted to catch him off his square. I also wanted to catch him anywhere near Kennedy, in any kind of sexual way, so that I had even more of a reason to murder his ass. I didn't give a fuck if they were just lying on the couch together; either way, the nigga was dead.

At the same time, I was reluctant to go inside. If Kennedy acted in any kind of way that she wanted to stay with this nigga, I wasn't prepared for that shit. I wasn't prepared to see Kennedy protect a man like she protected me. However, I couldn't be weak as fuck in front of my niggas, so as we left my car in the darkness of midnight and inched towards the home, I silently prayed that Kennedy was the same, loyal woman that had walked out on me. I prayed that she hadn't done the same as Jada and ran to another nigga to make her feel better. I prayed that this wasn't some nigga who was waiting on her to be released like I was. I prayed as I kicked at the front door, attempting to kick it down, but the anxiety and anticipation had me so fucking weak that I couldn't even kick that motherfucker down. We didn't want to attract the police by firing shots already before we got in, and we didn't have silencers this time. If you were from Chicago, you knew that this neighborhood was boogie as fuck and full of mostly white folks, so we had to be careful until we got to Kennedy and Kayla. So, Dolla was able to kick that motherfucker down just in time to see some nigga curiously rushing out of the kitchen. His eyes were wide as fuck as the three of us rushed into his home with guns drawn and pointed at his head. His hands were raised, but the nigga was looking at us with no alarm, like he knew exactly who we were.

"KING! What are you doing?!"

Even though this was a fucked up situation, seeing Kennedy after so long made a nigga's heart skip a couple of beats. She was obviously pissed off at me. The usual love and admiration that was usually in her eyes when she looked at me was gone. Now, she looked at me like I disgusted her, like she didn't know who the fuck I was.

"What the fuck are you doing here?" I barked. "Who is this nigga?"

"He's Ms. Jerry's grandson! Put them fuckin' guns down!" she shrieked. "Fuck is wrong wit' y'all? Damn!"

Meech and Dolla looked at me for confirmation. I shook my head, telling him and Meech not to let their guards down.

"Really, King?!" she spat.

I looked at her, questioning silently who the fuck she thought I was. If it wasn't for how much I knew she loved Ms. Jerry, I would have been put a bullet in this nigga just for him housing my bitch and my daughter.

"Yes, really! You know who the fuck I am! Stop acting brand new!" I snapped. "Let's go! Go get your shit!"

When she folded her arms stubbornly, I noticed what she was wearing. She only had on an oversized PINK sleep shirt that only fell a little ways past her waist. Most of her thick hips and thighs were exposed as she stood on the steps glaring at me. Nothing was on her feet.

She was comfortable in this nigga's crib. Real comfortable.

"You fuckin' this nigga?" I barked as I pointed the gun at him.

Kennedy raced towards me, noticing the fire in my eyes, the deadly look in them. "No, King!"

I continued to bark as I raced towards him with my gun pointed directly at his face. "Did you fuck her, nigga?"

He just stood there, saying nothing, not really giving a fuck about the anger in my eyes or the guns pointed at him.

"Like you was fucking, Siren? Huh?!" Kennedy spat as she attacked me, punching me in the back. But she was so much smaller than me that that shit didn't even hurt. But this nigga looked at Kennedy's hurt in concern, like he cared and wanted to shelter her. Seeing this nigga want to protect my woman; *that* hurt way more.

"Dolla, go find Kayla," I ordered.

"No!" Kennedy shouted. "Don't you fucking touch her, Dolla! We aren't leaving!"

Dolla ignored her and made his way up the stairs. Meech and I kept the guns on that lame ass nigga while Kennedy kept fussing. "Put the guns down, King! He's not going to do anything." Then she looked at him. "I'm so sorry, Glen."

Before he could respond, I snatched her by her arm. When she started to wrestle with me and I snatched her ass up, buddy acted like he wanted to come save her, but Meech cocked his pistol.

"Fuck you, King! I hate you! I'm never coming home with your lying ass!" She was smacking, kicking and punching her way out of my grasp but that shit wasn't fazing me.

Then I saw Dolla coming down the stairs with a sleeping Kayla in his arms. My nigga was thorough as fuck, he even had Kayla's baby bag and Kennedy's purse. Seeing my baby further let me know that I was taking my family home. Kennedy didn't have a choice; she was coming home.

I bent down and picked her up, throwing her over my shoulder like a sack of potatoes. I was so protective of every inch of her that I took the time to fix her nightshirt, covering her ass and legs as much as I could before walking towards the door.

"Put me down! I don't wanna go home with you!" Now, she was crying as I carried her out. Meech kept the gun on Glen until me and Dolla were out of the house with my precious cargo.

KENNEDY

I decided to stop screaming once we were outside. I didn't want to further embarrass myself in front of Glen by causing any of his neighbors to call the police, so I just stayed hoisted over King's shoulder as Dolla dug through my purse for my keys. After finding them and popping the lock, Dolla strapped Kayla in her car seat as King put me in the front seat and strapped me in as if I was just as young as Kayla.

"I got it!" I snapped as I snatched the seatbelt from him and fastened it myself. He looked at me with so much remorse and compassion. I could tell that I had hurt him by leaving, but fuck his feelings! I rolled my eyes and stared straight ahead.

In the past, I had never shown him any emotion but happiness and love. I'd had no reason to show him anything else. Now that I was giving him so much anger and grief for the first time, he sighed heavily and slammed the door. But I knew that he wasn't mad at me; he was mad at his gawd damn self.

He said a few words to Dolla and Meech before they got into the truck.

"I hate you," I sneered as soon as he got into the truck. But quickly my anger was replaced with hurt. I started to cry hysterically. "I swear to God, I hate you. I hate you for doing this to me."

My hands fell into my hands. I felt his hand soothingly on my thigh and rage quickly returned. I frantically smacked his hands away from me, as I screamed, "Don't touch me!"

He didn't even have any fight in him. He knew how bad he'd fucked up, so he didn't even bother to say anything. He just started the car and eased out of the driveway as I sat in the passenger side seat crying my eyes out.

"Kennedy, baby, I'm sorry. I'm sorry. I didn't know he was my son."

I was crying so hard that it felt like my throat would collapse. I didn't want to hear his explanation; that's why I just ran and never contacted him. Hearing him say sorry and hearing his explanation made this shit all the more real.

"Me...Me and Siren messed around here and there before I met you. It was just sex, never nothing more for me. Nobody knew that we fucked around. Not even Jada. That's why I didn't say shit when I met you. She was loyal to me by not ever saying shit to my peoples, so I did the same. I didn't tell Meech this, but she did have feelings for me. She wanted to be with me and did everything she could to be with me, but I never wanted her like that and never touched her again once I met you."

He sounded heartbroken as he finally, after the years, after all my sacrifice, told me the truth. I could imagine that it hurt him to tell me this because it was making him flawed in my eyes, when I once thought he was flawless. Because he was supposedly so loyal and honest with me, I was double that to him. He was no longer a king to me. He was regular, he was a peasant, just like these other niggas, and I knew that that broke his heart. But it wasn't even possible for him to hurt as much as I was.

I wasn't that naive. I knew that there were things that King had hidden from me. I knew that he wasn't perfect. But damn, not this! Not no shit like this!

"Baby?"

I couldn't stop crying long enough to answer him, nor did I want to answer him. I just wanted him to shut up. I just wanted him to stop talking so that I could stop dying inside. This shit was real. This shit *really* was happening. My nigga was really disloyal to me.

"Baby?"

"Just stop talking to me!" I cried. "Please stop talking to me!"

If I had had on shoes, I would have opened that car door and ran the moment he stopped at a red light. I hate to seem like I was being a punk because I just kept running, but I didn't know what the fuck else to do. I would have rather done three more years in prison than felt this shit right here.

"We have to talk about it, baby."

"I don't want to, King. Please just stop."

"Jada and the kids are at home, so we have to talk before we go in if you gon' be yelling and shit."

I looked at him curiously, asking, "Why is Jada and the kids there?"

He looked reluctant to tell me as he answered, "They've been staying there."

"Why?"

He sighed and replied, "I'll let her tell you."

I was so confused as he turned onto the block where our house was. I didn't want to go inside. I didn't want to be reminded of the words I heard when I walked into that kitchen a few weeks ago.

King was even hesitant as he pulled into the driveway. He turned the car off and sat in the seat, staring at nothing out of the window.

"I gotta tell you something else."

"Oh God," I groaned.

He ignored my reluctance. "Ummm... This detective has been on Siren for years, trying to get her to give her some information on me. It's some chick I fucked with ten years ago one night and never talked to her again. I guess she really got it out for me for whatever reason. Siren called herself giving her some information on a drop I was making a few years ago..." When he paused, his words sunk in and my eyes bulged. It was the first time I'd looked in his eyes since we got in the car.

Despite my reaction, he continued, "It was that drop you were making for me when-"

My sobs and heavy, sporadic breaths interrupted him. "So... so *Siren* is the reason why I got stopped that night? I went to jail because your old bitch was helping one of your other old bitches set you up?!"

I was losing my fucking mind. I had to be because this shit was crazy. It didn't feel real. Sitting in that car felt like a fucked up dream that I just wanted to wake up from.

I couldn't breathe. Shit, I thought him being Elijah's father hurt like a motherfucker. But, no, *this* shit hurt like a bitch.

I could barely hear King as he answered, "Yea... But I'm taking care of both of them, so you can't confront Siren about this. She doesn't know that we know any of this."

I stared aimlessly at nothing, feeling numb.

When I heard other cars pulling up, I knew that it was Meech and Dolla. This was my opportunity to get the fuck away from King, but this time, I wouldn't run without him knowing.

"I'm going to my mother's house." I heard him sigh long and hard so I added, "I don't want to be anywhere around you right now, King. I don't want to be in this relationship anymore, and I for damn sure don't want to be in the same house as you."

He sighed as he stuttered, "I-I understand but stay here. I'll go. Jada needs you anyway."

I was so curious as to what had happened with Jada that I didn't realize that King had left the car and started getting Kayla out of the backseat. I sat there thinking that he was right; I would be more comfortable at home without my mother shooting a hundred questions at me. So, I got out of the car, the pavement hot under my feet, the gravel sticking me in the bottom of my feet. King looked like he wanted to pick me up and carry me inside, but my eyes dared his ass to touch me. I could see Meech and Dolla standing outside of King's car, leaning against it as he followed me inside with Kayla, her bag and my purse in his hands.

"I'll put her down in her bed," King told me.

I let him, knowing that he had missed Kayla as much as he missed me. I looked around the house and noticed remnants of Bianca and Brandon everywhere, despite the fact that the housecleaner had been there. I knew she had; I could smell her signature air freshener in the air. Before going to find Jada, I went into the kitchen, found the pain medicine in the cabinets and took four, 200mg Ibuprofens.

"I need some fucking muscle relaxers or something," I mumbled.

I left the kitchen and felt as if I was floating upstairs. I was having an out-of-body experience or some shit. This shit just could not be real.

As I walked past Kayla's room, I saw King lying in bed with her, holding her as she slept and continuously kissing her face. I kept walking, noticing a TV on in one of the guest bedrooms. I crept down the hall, careful not to make too much noise because I knew the kids were asleep somewhere nearby. I slowly pushed the door open and saw Jada lying in bed, staring at the television with tears in her eyes. When she saw me, her eyes bucked but there was no happiness to see me.

"What's wrong?" I asked as I rushed in.

Instantly, sobs accompanied her tears. "Where the fuck you been?"

I ran towards her, asking, "What happened to you?"

"Fuck you, bitch. I needed you. Where you been?" She meant every curse word she was saying, but she was sad more than anything, so I didn't take offense to any of them as I climbed into bed with my own tears streaming down my face.

"I'm sorry. I heard King and Meech talking. I found out that Elijah was King's son-"

"I know. King told me."

"I couldn't take that shit. I had to bounce."

"I understand that, but, bitch, I needed you. You could have called me. I wouldn't have told King where you were. Fuck him. Fuck all of them niggas."

"*What happened*, Jada?"

She took a deep breath and sat up in bed. She shook her head and sneered as the thought came to mind. "The same thing that happened to you."

I looked at her with even more questions in my eyes.

"Dolla showed up at the crib like a week and a half ago with two kids..." My mouth dropped and my eyes bulged as she continued, "Twins, bitch. Apparently, their mother died in a car accident that night, so he had to bring them home."

My mouth fell open even further. "Oh my God! I'm so sorry, Jada."

"That nigga never said one word about getting a bitch pregnant. He made me feel like I was being crazy every time I told him that I knew he was up to something. He probably was never going to tell me about those fucking babies."

"So you left him?"

"Hell yea, I left him, tried to shoot him, *and* stabbed him."

This time when my mouth dropped, it was accompanied with a chuckle. "You did what?"

"It's been bad, girl," she replied as she reached for a cup on her nightstand. "It's been real bad. You want some?" Then she shoved the cup in my face. It smelled like whiskey, and I had to hold back the automatic gag reflex. After drinking that Hennessy with Glen the night before, I woke up the next morning sick as hell. This baby was totally rejecting alcohol to the point that it had me throwing up everything that morning.

"No, I can't drink."

I hadn't even noticed how I answered her until she looked at me like I was crazy.

I quickly added, "I already feel like shit. Liquor is just going to make it worse."

She shrugged and took a big gulp. That's when I noticed a bruise on her face. "What happened to your face? Did Dolla hit you?"

As she answered, through the doorway, I noticed King leaving our bedroom with a large duffel bag in his hand. He went down the stairs, and then it was official; he was letting me have the house without any argument. I didn't know how I felt about that. No matter what he said, I didn't want to be with him anymore, but I still wanted the nigga to fight for me. Silly, I know, but it made me feel better to see him grovel.

My attention was quickly taken from King to Jada as she started to tell me about going out with Marcus and him kidnapping her, beating her and actually wanting a ransom. When she told me how Dolla treated her, after finding out that she'd fucked Marcus, I was floored, and somewhat relieved. You always think you're going through hell until you hear someone else's fucked up story and find out that your situation can be so much worse.

"Oh my God, Jada," I said as I put my arm around her, trying to soothe her tears.

"We hate each other, girl. Just that quick, all the years we spent together is over. What am I gon' do? Where am I going to work? I have never even been to college, never had a real job. How am I going to take care of these kids, girl?"

I didn't have an answer for her, so I just shook my head with sadness. Shit, I was wondering the same about myself. King nor Dolla would ever leave us out here that bad, but now, being single mothers, we were going to have to do a lot of things on our own that we never had to before.

"Girl, this shit is just crazy. Everything is falling apart," Jada said sadly. "I hate Dolla."

"I hate King...and Siren."

Jada snarled. "I despise that bitch. Oh! Let me tell you about that too."

Jada started to spill some tea that left me speechless! She told me about everything that had happened and how she had kept it all from me because she didn't want to ruin my wedding with the bullshit. She told me about Meech telling her to go find Siren, about how she found Siren talking to a detective and shot her, and all the threats Siren had been making since then.

I couldn't believe this snake bitch had been in our midst and none of us had a clue! I was so pissed off at King, and didn't even want to think about him, but I had faith that he was truly taking care of this bitch once and for all, and I couldn't wait.

MEECH

I shook my head, taking another shot. "This shit crazy."

"As hell," Dolla sighed, shaking his head.

"Fa sho," King responded as he nodded sadly and slowly.

We were some of the richest niggas in the Chi, but as we sat at the bar at Gibson's Steakhouse, we were looking pathetic as hell and broke down. But while these two niggas were salty over losing their women, I was salty that mine was still in my house!

"Where you gon' stay, bruh?" Dolla asked King.

King shrugged, saying, "I don't know. All my properties have tenants in them-"

"And my agent just told me that somebody finally got approved for my condo and signed the lease."

King shrugged. "Guess I'll go get a hotel until I have time to buy me something."

"Buy you something?" I repeated in disbelief. King sounded like he and Kennedy were really over, and it would be real fucked up if he lost that girl over Siren's lying ass. "You and Kennedy through for real?"

I had never seen the nigga so sad. Wait... Nah, I seen that nigga that sad when I approached him about Elijah. He was fucked up then, and he was even more fucked up now.

"She hate me, bruh. Not only was I dishonest about my relationship with Siren, I got the son with Siren that I wanted to have with Kennedy. Then Kennedy went to jail behind this bitch... I don't see how she'll ever forgive me for this."

We all sat in silence. Dolla and Jada breaking up was one thing. As his boys, King and I saw him do some really foul shit to Jada over the years. Some shit she knew about, some shit she didn't. So, we all knew that nigga had one foot out of the door and didn't deserve a down ass bitch like Jada. It was to no surprise that all of his bullshit had come back to smack him in the face. Shit, even when she was in that crib fucking that nigga I didn't blame Jada at all. And me and Siren; the shit she did was so foul that I *had* to get rid of that bitch. There was no question. But King and Kennedy were the couple to emulate. They were the Beyoncé and Jay of the hood. They were the Teyana Taylor and Iman Shumpert of the ghetto. They were the hood's Barack and Michelle. Everybody wanted a love like theirs. Shit, even me. King may have had a fucked up sense of loyalty some years ago, but I was man enough to see that he had spent time since then making that shit up to me and Kennedy. I hated to see Kennedy lose her family because of a mistake that King made before they met, just to then end up with a nigga like Dolla.

"How long Gustavo say we gotta wait to handle this shit with Siren, man?" I asked.

Dolla chuckled. "You tired of frontin' for that bitch?"

I huffed. "Man, joe, that shit is killin' me."

"Not that much longer," King told me. "He's just taking the steps to make sure that this shit goes right. Now that we made it look like Siren set Maria up, we should have bought ourselves some time. Maria shouldn't trust Siren now, and she's hopefully staying away from her...What's up with London? Did she like the truck?"

I shrugged my shoulders, realizing how heavy they felt. "I guess."

On top of Siren's presence in my crib irritating the fuck outta me, I felt bad as hell that London wasn't letting me fix this shit between us. I missed shorty. Shit, it wasn't even about the pussy; I missed just hanging out and having a drink with her. But the truck really was something for her with no strings attached. I felt like shit having Siren's bitch ass in my crib sucking up all the free air, food and roof, when London's sweet ass was walking to the bus stop every day. I didn't feel like a real nigga with her walking. Even though she wasn't fucking with me no more, I had had the pussy once, so being a man, I had to get her off that bus.

Dolla sucked his teeth. "You guess? Shit, anything is betta than being on feet. A new truck definitely is."

King chuckled. "Real talk."

"She likes it, I'm sure. She just didn't want to take it at first. She think I'm trying to buy her pussy or some shit."

Dolla shook his head as if he couldn't believe London's response. "She ain't never met a real nigga."

I looked at Dolla like he was crazy. It was the wrong time for him to be bragging about being a "real nigga," and he knew it.

"Aye," he said defensively. "My situation is different. I tried to spare my bitch. The universe made me tell her the way that I did. I didn't want to hurt her like that, man."

"So strap up when you fuck around on her, nigga," King told him. "That's street nigga 101, and that's 'real nigga' shit. You don't bring no babies to the crib."

Dolla cocked his head to the side and looked at King like he was the one crazy as fuck now. I started cracking up laughing!

"Aye, Elijah was before Kennedy, and I didn't even know," King told us.

Dolla nodded. "True, true."

I grabbed another shot from the twenty shots we'd ordered when we walked in and threw it back. "Fuck it. We're all fuck ups," I told them. "We all got some shit to learn about loving these chicks."

CHAPTER TWELVE

MEECH

A couple of hours later, we were all stumbling out of the bar. Since Dolla and I had rode together, King offered to take him home. Then, I took my drunk ass to London's mother's house unannounced. I just couldn't go home. I didn't want to, and I didn't want to be anywhere but with London, so that's where I went, knowing that she would show her ass for me showing up at three in the morning. That's what I was expecting when I pulled up. What I *wasn't* expecting was to see her phat ass leaning against a Chrysler 300 with some nigga in her face.

I flung my door open and jumped out before my ride was even in park. When I felt the truck still moving, I had to jump back in, throw it in park and hop back out, leaving the door open, as I stormed towards London and this sucka ass nigga. London was already on guard, looking at me wide-eyed as she stood in front of him as if she was protecting this nigga. And his bitch ass let her. I don't know what pissed me off more; her being with a nigga or her being with a punk ass nigga.

Like I said, I was tipsy already, so I allowed my anger to convince me into pulling my piece out on this motherfucka.

"Nigga, if you wanna live, leave."

London gasped. "You got a lot of fucking nerve! Did I show up at your door making motherfuckas leave? Oh, no, I didn't because I don't know *where the fuck you live* since you live with a woman!"

This nigga hadn't moved yet, and it was pissing me the fuck off. I looked at London and calmly told her, "Shut up." Her mouth dropped, but I ignored her dramatics. I cocked my pistol. I aimed it past her and straight at this nigga as I told him, "Don't die over no pussy, especially this one, 'cause it's mine. Bounce, my nigga."

This goofy motherfucka looked like he was pissing in his pants as he eased London to the side and got in his car.

"I can't believe you!" she shrieked.

"I can't believe you fuckin' with a nigga like that. What the fuck was that nigga wearin'? Skinny jeans? Driving this whack ass 300!" I snapped as I kicked the door while he drove away.

"MEECH!" she yelled.

"WHAT?!"

My anger was alarming her, so as this goofy drove away, I took a deep breath. "You gave up on me already? You already on to the next nigga?"

"See? That's why I didn't want that fucking truck! You don't own me!"

I walked up on her, grabbing her ass and pulling her into me. "I own that pussy though."

I had the effect on her that I wanted to have. I could see her breath shorten and quicken. I could literally see the goosebumps on her light skin. But she fought away the lust that I had just drilled into her.

She pushed me away. "You're crazy!"

Staring into her eyes, I licked my lips. "For you, yea."

"How can you be crazy about me? Does she still live with you?"

I didn't answer because I didn't want to hurt her with the truth or a lie, so I just looked at her.

She shook her head with a look of disgust in her eyes. "See? You probably fuck that bitch every night."

"I swear I don't."

She sucked her teeth. "Yea right."

"I'll sit out here every night to show you that I'm not, if it makes you feel better."

She looked at me as if she didn't believe a word I said. "I have to go to work in a few hours. I don't have time for this shit."

She walked away, and I let her.

I didn't fight with her partly because I knew she was right. I was bogus as hell for sending her off, for not telling the truth about Siren. But I also didn't argue with her because I enjoyed the sight of her walking away from me, the jiggle of her phat ass, the voluptuousness of her body, every dimple, every curve. But the door slamming brought me out of my trance, and I reluctantly walked towards my truck. I got in and made myself comfortable in the driver's seat, leaning back.

If she needed proof that I wasn't fucking Siren, that was what she was going to get.

DOLLA

After King dropped me off at my car, I decided to ride down on one of my old dips. I thought she wouldn't answer since I hadn't fucked with her in so long. My mind had been so wrapped up in Meagan, Jada, and the twins. Plus, a nigga was trying to do right by his girl and his family, so I had gone MIA on shorty. But since Jada wanted to be out in these streets thottin' around, a nigga was about to get him some action and not feel guilty about it for once.

Just like in the past, as soon as I called shorty, she picked up, but I could hear the attitude in her voice as she answered.

"What you want, Dolla?"

"You," I answered flatly.

She sucked her teeth and blew her breath, giving me a whole lot of attitude. "Is that right? And what you want from me?"

"You know what I want. That's why you answered the phone at four o'clock in the morning." Then I chuckled, trying to lighten her mood, but it didn't work. She knew I was on bullshit, but bullshit smells like Chanel No5 when coming from the lips of the nigga you've been wanting to make that hotline bling.

I'd met Tay at Brazzar's about three years ago. She was a boogie looking chick in a pencil skirt and blazer. She was looking thick as fuck, yet beautifully classy, and a nigga was intrigued. I was surprised when she stepped to a nigga like me. I was wearing baggy jeans and a hoody, but a street nigga like me being in such a classic steakhouse such as Brazzar's probably told her that I was nothing but money. Still, when she told me that she was a scientist at a chemical plant, I didn't even bother stepping to her established ass, gave her a little conversation, bought her a drink and went to my table with my niggas. I admired her for being a successful, independent woman, but a nigga with a family couldn't be shit to a woman like that...I thought. I assumed women like her required more than what I was willing to give, but lo and behold, she sent me a bottle to the table with a note that had her number on it, and before even learning her last name, I was deep in her pussy that night.

Tay was an educated, well-paid thot, but still a thot.

"Whatever, motherfucker. Now all of a sudden you want this pussy, when you been dodging me for damn near a year?"

"Come on, ma. I told you I was trying to do right by my girl."

"Okay, and? Why are you calling me now then?"

Even at four o'clock in the morning, even in my drunken state of mind, it fucked me up when I said, "I ain't got no girl no more."

I couldn't believe how real that shit was, how final the shit felt. Me and Jada really were through; we really weren't a family anymore. This shit was crazy.

But as Tay told me, with a voice that was now much more flirtatious and inviting, "You sound sad about that, but I can make you feel so much better," my sadness quickly went away. I was willing to fuck the anger away if shorty let me.

"You on your way?" she asked.

Goofy ass bitch, I thought as I said, "Yea, baby. Get it ready for this dick too."

She giggled, replying, "Okay."

I shook my head as I hung up and made my way to her side of town. I couldn't believe how goofy some women were willing to be just for the chance of getting some dick and attention. Women were always screaming about what they won't take from a man but are willing to demean and belittle themselves for the smallest amount of attention. A man can't have Netflix & Chill without a woman okay'ing it. A nigga can't put a woman in a "situationship" without her okay'ing it. I didn't want Jada turning into one of those goofy ass broads that a nigga ran up in in the middle of the night, or one of those women that constantly got played, but unfortunately, it seemed like she was turning into just that. That's why I was losing respect for her faster than I was about to bust this nut in this thot.

I know I was being hypocritical like a motherfucker, but Jada knew that she had to walk a fine line. She was my woman, Dolla's woman. She couldn't be out here doing dicks recklessly. She couldn't be out here trusting any ol' nigga. Marcus was proof of that shit. Jada knew better. She was right in the streets with me for over eight years, so she knew how the game went. I was super disappointed in her for slippin' like that.

Not even ten minutes later, I was on the elevator in a high rise on Dearborn Street.

Just as I made it the twenty-third floor, a fucked up feeling swam through my stomach. I wanted to blame it on the liquor, but drunk or not, I knew that it was something else. It was guilt. The shit that I was doing was what got me in the fucked up position that I was in now. Fucking bitches was what led me to losing my family, and could even be why Meagan was dead, because who knows where she would have been that day if she had never met me. Hell, I was pissed off at Jada for fucking that nigga, but I even had sense enough to know that, had I not broke her heart, she would have been with me and not laid up with some nigga that was just setting up her vulnerable ass.

"You okay?"

I hadn't even realized that Tay had opened the door. I looked up and was surprised to see that she was completely naked. Her pussy looked as smooth as silk, her titties were juicy and perky, and her small waist dipped in so tiny that it made her hips look enormous and were a perfect match to her phat ass. Her natural twist out was falling on her shoulders and into her eyes, which were flirtatiously staring into me.

"I gotta go," I answered.

Her eyes squinted curiously and she frowned. "What? Why?"

I turned to walk away, and she actually stepped out into the hallway, grabbing my arm slightly. I was so frustrated, so pissed off with myself that I snatched away so hard that it made her lose her balance. Her eyes bulged as she braced herself against the wall.

"Let me go, bitch," I spat as I walked away.

I was bogus; I knew this. I was mad at myself, not her. But I couldn't be sensitive in front of this chick, so I had to lash out at her so that she would let me ride out in as much peace as possible.

"Fuck you, Dolla!"

I kept walking onto the elevator, allowing the door to close on her "you ain't shits" and "fuck yous."

KENNEDY

"You okay?"

I was laid back on my bed with a smile on my face. It was the first time that I smiled since King had dragged me out of Glen's house like King-fucking-Kong.

"Yeah, I'm okay," I told Glen as my smile flowed through my lips and into the phone.

"Good. Sounds like you're smiling."

"I am...now."

"Oh really?" was accompanied with a seductive, charming chuckle that made me squeeze my knees together tightly.

"Yea," I sighed. "Really."

I knew what I was feeling, and there was no confusion about it. There was something about Glen's protection that just made me feel so normal, like I used to feel before King's bullshit was revealed. What Glen made me feel was how King used to make me feel. The night that I tried to sleep with Glen was a huge mistake. It wasn't real. I didn't want him; I wanted King. Besides my hormones speaking for me, I was lashing out and reaching out for King.

"Good," Glen said. "Keep in touch."

"I definitely will. Thank you for putting up with me and Kayla for so long. And I am so sorry about King and his crew coming into your house like that."

"I don't blame the man. I would have done it to get you back to me too. I wouldn't let you go either."

I forced back a grin and ignored the throbbing in my clitoris. "That's sweet."

"That's *truth*... Talk to you later."

"Bye."

With a huge sigh, I ended the call while avoiding Jada's eyes.

"Bitch, who was that?!"

I laughed into my pillow. "That was Glen."

"Oh, your beau."

As Jada and I lay in bed all day - crying, complaining, venting, crying again, eating and watching *Snapped*, *Fatal Attraction* and any other show that was about a woman killing her man - I told her about me spazzing and trying to fuck Glen.

"That is not my beau."

"Shiiiid, I can't tell by that smile you had on your face. You like him."

"He is fine as fuck, with money, caring, sensitive and all that sexy ass shit that these hood ass, street niggas aren't; of course, I like him. Plus, he was missing his girl, while I was walking my phat ass around his house in t-shirts, so of course he was attracted to me. He never acted on it, though. I was the one being a thot." I cringed at the thought.

"You were trying to rebound, just like me. At least you didn't end up in bed with a nigga that was just setting you up."

I looked sadly at Jada, who was next to me on her back, looking up at the ceiling and shaking her head in disgust. "I can't believe I laid there, letting that motherfucker beat my ass because I was protecting Dolla, and then Dolla wouldn't even fucking answer the phone. I don't give a fuck if he was mad at me or what I've done to him. I am the mother of his kids. Anything could have happened to me or our kids and the nigga didn't even answer the fucking phone." She sighed deeply as she wiped away a lonely tear. "I've been more loyal to him than anybody else in my life; even my mother and my kids. But this nigga wouldn't even answer the damn phone."

I watched Jada's pain intently. Dolla had been shitting on her for years. She forgave him over and over again, and now look at her; she was lying there, lifeless; the only thing keeping her from taking herself out to cure the pain was her children. I didn't want to be her. I didn't want to forgive King, continue to be his woman and have his babies while he took my forgiveness as stupidity and weakness and kept shitting on me.

Jada's pain was further confirmation that I was *not* having this baby. No way. As I was thinking about how I would sneak to have an abortion, I heard her ask, "Has King been calling you?"

"Hell yea," I answered as I sucked my teeth. I sneered just thinking about it. King had been calling me nonstop since he left the day before, but all he had been telling me was a bunch of nothing that didn't make this shit feel better at all. I knew that he was sorry; that was no question. But sorry didn't fix this shit right here; not at all.

"What is he saying?"

"Nothing that fucking explains why he never told me that he used to fuck with Siren."

"I still can't believe that shit. That bitch been faking the whole time we been friends it seems like. I can't believe she never told me. What type of shit is that?"

I lay next to Jada simmering in my rage. Siren was lucky that I respected King's wishes about not confronting her. Otherwise, her ass would have been answering my questions with my foot kicking her fucking teeth down her throat. "I don't know what to be madder at; the fact that they never said anything about fucking around or the fact that the bitch was the reason why I went to prison."

Jada sighed long, loud and deeply. "Be mad at it all. This shit is fucked up."

"Definitely. It's most definitely fucked up."

SIREN

"Damn, girl, you look good," I told myself as I admired my body in the full-length mirror in the guest bedroom.

My voluptuous body was draped in nearly nothing. After bathing, I had gone into my closet and pulled out some lingerie pieces that I used to wear to blow Meech's mind. The one I was currently wearing I hadn't been able to show him before all hell broke loose. But tonight was *the* night. I was wearing a Tropic Rose, lace teddie. The overall lace highlighted every inch of my light-brown skin. The deep plunge neckline overly exposed my juicy titties. My big ass booty was swallowing the thong back. To add some sexiness -not that I needed anymore- I threw on a pair of five-inch stiletto peep toe pumps. My hair was pulled up into a high bun to prevent any of the twenty-eight inches from hiding a centimeter of my body.

Meech may have been able to avoid this pussy for the last two weeks, but not for too much longer. I was starting to think that he wasn't fucking me because he was still getting it from that light-skinned bitch, London. That feeling got worse when he spent the night out last night. I was still walking on eggshells around him, so I wasn't going to go through his phone or follow him in order to find out. I couldn't risk doing shit else to piss him off. I would be out on the street. However, I knew that once I was sucking and fucking that dick on a regular basis again, he would start to remember how things were before I fucked up everything, and I would be his girl again.

Shit! I thought as I heard my text message notification going off. Maria had a special notification, so I knew it was her. She had been sending me threatening text messages since the day we got shot at in the Walmart parking lot. She was convinced that I had set her up to be killed and was hitting me with every threat she had.

"Fuck that bitch," I muttered as I continued to admire myself in the mirror. I would worry about Maria later. Tonight, my focus was on Meech.

Since I had sent Meech a text asking what time he'd be home to eat the dinner I'd cooked, I knew that he would be walking through the door any second, so I pranced downstairs. I tiptoed past Elijah's room in order not to wake him. Then I went into the kitchen, made me a Long Island, and then turned off the light and left. I had lied to Meech; there was no dinner. *I* was the dinner. I wanted that nigga to eat me all night. If he really needed to eat some food, that nigga could use Grubhub. I had been letting this nigga be mad long enough; it was time for me to use what I had to get what I wanted. And Meech was what I wanted. He was what I needed.

Once inside of the living room, which was in sight of the front door, I turned on the surround sound and played some slow jams. Then, I waited.

CHAPTER THIRTEEN

MEECH

I felt a little foolish after waking up that morning in my car to see that London had left for work without even saying anything to me after I had slept outside of her crib like some type of ghetto, pathetic Romeo all night. But I knew that she saw that I was out there, and that was all that mattered. She was playing hard to get, but I was down for the challenge. I wanted her to know that I was down for her for real, that I truly was a really good dude, and that I was sincerely sorry, so I was back the next night to sleep outside of her house like a complete gump.

Now it was the next night. It was around midnight, and all my business had been taken care of, I was ready to get some rest, but as soon as I pulled up, London came storming out of her house.

I chuckled as London looked at me like I was a fool while she stood outside of my car.

"What are you doin' here?" I heard her ask on the other side of the window.

With a smile, I rolled the window down. "I'm doing to bed."

She sucked her teeth and shook her head. "You can't sleep out here again. These niggas gon' jack you."

"Girl, I run these motherfuckin' streets. Ain't nobody gon' fuck with me."

Her head cocked to the side as she peered through the window. "Go home."

"No. Since you think I'm sleeping with her every night, I'm showing you that I'm not."

London shook her head again as her eyes rolled into the back of her head.

"You look nice." She did for real. All she had on was a fitted, plain, t-shirt dress, but that shit looked like Gucci on her. "Where you comin' from?"

She had accidentally relaxed. She was about to answer my question until she checked herself. "Unt uh! You don't get to ask me where I'm coming from!"

I shrugged. "Have it your way, baby. Whatever you want."

We held eye contact for a few seconds. Never thought I would use a word like this before, but that shit was *electrifying* ... Yea, it was electrifying, and the voltage went straight to my dick. She felt that shit too, but she was still being stubborn.

"Bye, Meech," she said before leaving the window.

"Bye, baby."

"I'm not your baby!" she shot over her shoulder as she stomped through the yard.

Seeing that ass jiggle as she struggled to walk fast in those flip-flops was every-fucking-thing.

Fuck.

My phone rang, interrupting my eye-fucking session, and I knew who it was. Ever since I had spent the night out the night before, Siren had been on my bumper. This wasn't part of the plan. I was supposed to play her close until our plan played out, but I had to show London what she meant to me, so I was just going to have to take that risk.

I silenced my phone, leaned the seat back and sparked my blunt, ready to end my night.

SIREN

What the hell?

I looked around the living room wondering what time it was. I noticed the sun peeking through the window, and my heart sank, realizing that Meech must not have ever come home. I looked at my phone, and there were no missed calls from him, despite the fact that I had called him, at least, ten times before I obviously fell asleep against my will. Embarrassed, I quickly stood and ran up the steps, hoping that Elijah didn't wake up to see his mom dressed like a stripper at five o'clock in the morning.

Assuming that Meech was up under London was making a very familiar feeling surface beneath my skin. This nigga was choosing this high-yellow bitch over his family, and I was too be damned if I was going to allow it to happen. I had been playing it cool for way too long. I was playing it so cool to the point that my cool ass was going to lose my man to this bitch. I was to be damned if she was going to be in my bedroom, the bedroom that he still hadn't let me back into! She was now on my list of bitches that had to go!

Once inside of my room, I slammed the door and started to change while dialing out on me cell phone. Of course, I was calling Meech. I did not care that I had already called him ten times before. I didn't care how crazy I looked. I *wanted* him to know that I was crazy. He probably had me in check to a certain extent; I wasn't about to go around poppin' up at places and fighting his hoes anymore. However, he was *not* going to play me. He was not going to be in the house acting like a family man, but spending the night out.

"Urgh!"

When Meech didn't answer, I got so fucking frustrated that I tossed my phone across the room. Then my crazy ass realized that I wanted to shoot him a text message, so I ran after it and snatched it up.

Me: Elijah is starting to wonder why you haven't been home at night. What am I supposed to tell him? We're still a family, Meech. Since when did you start spending the night out? Is her pussy that good?

After pressing send, I quickly dialed another number.

"Hello?" she had answered as if she wanted to reach through the phone and smack the shit out of me; maybe even shoot me a couple of times again.

But I completely ignored her attitude, like I didn't even hear that shit. "Hey, girl. Are you with Dolla? Did he come home last night?"

Jada sucked her teeth. "Girl, what the hell are you doing asking me some shit like this at five o'clock in the morning? Bitch, didn't I tell that we're not friends?! Get the fuck off my phone!"

Again, I was so obsessed with knowing where the fuck Meech was that I ignored her. I just really wanted some confirmation that Meech wasn't falling for this bitch. I didn't need that shit. "Are the guys together? I'm looking for Meech."

"*Bitch*, I don't fuck with you!" Jada squealed. "Don't get it twisted. Don't think we still friends because I ain't told nobody your business. Get the fuck off my line."

Then I heard dead air, so I tore the phone away from my ear and saw that the call had ended.

"Aaargh!"

JADA

Siren's phone call early that morning wasn't the only fucked up call that I'd gotten that day. It seemed as if she and Dolla insisted on fucking up every day that I still breathed.

It took everything in me not to say some slick shit after hanging up on Dolla. Since Brandon was in the room, and he was so in his feelings about being away from his father, I had to watch my tongue.

Kennedy saw the look on my face and told Brandon, "Hey, Brandon. Why don't you go upstairs and get dressed so we can go get you guys something to eat?"

He sucked his teeth and told Kennedy, "But I'm not hungry."

My eyes shot towards him like knives. "Boy, don't you fucking talk back to her! If she said go upstairs, take your little ass upstairs right now before I beat the shit out of you."

He did as he was told, but he still did it with a gawd damn attitude. He huffed and puffed and stomped out of the living room. When I tried to get up to snatch his little ass up, Kennedy quickly grabbed my arm and sat me back down, giving me a warning look.

"I'm going to fuck Brandon up. He is doing the most. I don't feel like this shit," I said as I ran my fingers through my hair. I was so pissed off that my eyes were burning from oncoming tears, and my leg was bouncing up and down nervously.

"He just misses his father, Jada. You know that."

I did know that. Which was why when Dolla called, asking me if his kids could come over for a few days because he missed them being in the house, I agree. But as soon as I heard those little bastard ass kids in the background whining, I spazzed and hung up on his ass.

"Can you believe that that son of a bitch wants my kids to be around those babies like we're going to be some big ass happy family? He got me fucked up!"

Kennedy looked at me reluctantly before saying, "Jada, I really don't think that that's a bad idea-"

She stopped talking as soon as I gave her the look of death as I asked her, "Are you fucking serious?"

"I'm only saying that because you need a break. You can't handle these kids in the state of mind that you're in right now. You need a break."

"But those fucking babies are there!"

"And they're going to be there, Jada. They aren't going anywhere-"

"It's just too soon, Kennedy."

"It may be too soon for you, but the kids have nothing to do with that. They miss Dolla, especially Brandon. It was obvious that they missed being at home. And you are about to fucking lose it if they keep getting on your nerves. Let him take them for a couple of days. Since he over there playing daddy with those twins, let him play daddy with these kids too." That was the truth. I needed a break before I wound up hurting somebody. I was spazzing out on my kids, screaming at the top of my lungs at the littlest things. Brandon was even starting to lash out a little bit because he missed his daddy.

"Fine. I'll drop them off. But you're coming with me."

Kennedy laughed. "That's fine. I might need to come anyway to keep you from trying to kill Dolla...again."

****

An hour later, we were in Kennedy's Bentley truck pulling up to the house I used to share with Dolla. When I first left with my children a couple of weeks ago, no matter how mad I was, I really thought that I would be returning one day. I was returning now but not like I thought I was. I thought I would be coming back in preparation to continue to live with my man and my family like nothing ever happened. I thought that Dolla would work his way back into my heart with apologies, flowers, and anything he had to do to get me back, but that has not been the case. I was coming back to drop my kids off in order to give their part-time dad visitation for a few days.

I never thought our family would have come to this.

"Go on Brandon and Brittany. Be careful getting out of the car and take all of your bags with you."

Brandon got out of the car so fast that he damn near tripped.

"Didn't I say be careful? Slow down, Brandon!"

But Brandon wasn't listening. He was so excited to see his father that he raced towards the front door. Brittany, on the other hand, was taking her sweet time. She knew that her father had done something to hurt me, and she was smart enough to realize that it had a lot to do with the two babies that her father was holding when he opened the door for Brandon.

When Kennedy and I noticed him in the doorway, Kennedy let out a deep sigh, looked sympathetically into my eyes, and put her hand on my knee.

She asked me, "Are you okay?"

"Is this shit real?" That was a legit question because I swear this shit didn't feel real. I felt like I was in a scary movie or something. Life felt eerie right about now. Seemingly, all my life I had been with this man. I woke up to him, went to sleep to him, loved him, fought with him, fought *for* him, cried with him, cried over him... and now we were nothing? We weren't even acknowledging each other?

When Kennedy sighed so deeply that she caught my attention, I felt how wet my face was. I hadn't even realized that

I was crying as I stared out of the window towards the house that I fucking decorated.

I was so glad that the windows in Kennedy's truck were tinted.

I sighed deeply and stared at those babies. I stared at those twins, wondering how something so small could ruin the rest of my life. I couldn't understand how two little people had the power to take everything from me. Since I had first laid eyes on them, I had not been the same woman. It wasn't fair that their existence in this world had ended mine.

Dolla didn't even acknowledge me. He didn't even attempt to come to the truck and speak, to ask if I was okay, or if I even needed anything. Just a couple of weeks ago, I was his end all and be all. Even though I knew he was cheating on me, I was, at least, a factor in his life. Making one mistake, choosing to do me for once in eight years, had caused me to be a none-motherfucking-factor in his life, a life that I had bent over backward to help him create, just that quick. He had made thousands of mistakes. However, I had held on for eight years. I had forgiven him for eight years and had never left his side; not once, not even for a day. I took care of him, looked after him and helped him build his future, more than I had even done for myself. And this was the thanks that I got; a broken family, no man, and no forgiveness.

I sighed hard, attempting to get myself together, and wiped the two tears away that had fallen as I solemnly watched Dolla usher the children into the house.

"I'm okay," I finally answered Kennedy, "But let's get the fuck out of here before I catch a case."

KENNEDY

I guess me and Jada's situation was different. Although King had for sure broken my heart into many pieces, I respected his gangsta way too much to keep him away from his daughter. It was easier for me to do it at Glen's house because I wasn't in King's presence. But now that I was in our home that he built for us, I respected the man enough to let him come over and have his family time. So after we left Dolla's and had a bite to eat, King met me back at our home. Jada jumped in her car and decided to go spend some time with her mother.

"Daddy? Why you don't live here no more?"

I felt like shit, and so did King. His sexy ass eyes lowered to the ground like a coward. He couldn't even look Kayla in the eyes as he said, "I still live here, baby. I'm just ..." He hesitated, not knowing what to say. I saw him fighting a battle within himself, trying to figure out something to tell his daughter that made sense to her smart ass. "I just don't feel good, and I don't want to get you all sick. Okay?"

"But you don't look sick, daddy."

King sighed and picked her up. "Daddy is sick on the inside, babe."

I looked at them both as they stood next to the island in the kitchen. King sat Kayla in her highchair. He then made her plate, cutting up the Beggar's pizza that he'd brought with him into tiny pieces.

As I watched him, I was mad as hell that he had ruined this picture for me. I once looked at him and felt so grateful for everything that I had. I mean, who had a man like mine? I never thought that any other woman had a man like King; a man that could tell her that the sky was pink, and she could have all faith that he was telling her the truth. Hell, King could have told me that my name was actually Tiana, and I would have believed him because *that's* how honest I thought he had been with me. I used to look at King and see perfection. I used to look at him and see the perfect ghetto fantasy. He was the ideal Clyde to my Bonnie.

He just had to go and fuck all of that up! I risked my life for that phony ass picture that he planted in my head. I felt so stupid for doing that time without ever questioning anything.

King must have thought that my thoughts were going there because he sat beside me with two plates full of sausage and pepperoni pizza with extra cheese, onions, and green peppers. That bastard had gotten my favorite food, not even knowing that this baby inside of me had been craving it for two days.

I began to stuff my face, ignoring the sympathetic eyes that he was staring at me with. I was so busy being a fat ass that I was vulnerable when I felt his hand tenderly rubbing the back of my neck as he told me, "I really miss you."

I wanted to tell him, "I miss you too," because I really did. Like I said, me and Jada's situations were different. I didn't feel as much volatile anger towards King because this was his first offense, that I knew of. Jada wanted to kill Dolla because he had done this to her so many times and gotten her forgiveness, just for him to do that shit again and be so reckless that he had ultimately made the worst mistake of Jada's life. King had done the same; he had made the worst mistake of my life as well, but I didn't have as much hate in my heart as Jada, not so much hate that it outweighed the fact that I truly did miss my man.

However, the nigga had to suffer, so I was not about to fall into his embrace or those three words that he felt would fix what he had fucked up. So, I simply nodded and kept eating, but I didn't move his hand away as he continued to touch the back of my neck and my hair.

****

A few hours later, we were in the middle of an animated movie marathon with Kayla. King had suggested that we all watch it together in bed, and of course, Kayla agreed because she loved to lie in bed with mommy and daddy. But I side-eyed King because I knew he was up to something. That was confirmed when he left during the trailers of Frozen and came back with two drinks in hand, one for me and one for him. I was so stressed being in that room and in the bed with him again that I absentmindedly took the drink and gulped it down. I mean, I was torn between hating this nigga, never wanting to see him again, wanting him to spend those three years in prison that I did, since I did that shit for no reason, and missing the shit out of him, wanting to be in his arms, wanting to be back in a relationship with him, and acting like this shit never happened. So, yeah, I was stressed, and the only thing that would make the shit go away quickly and make these movies go by faster was drinking.

But I should have known that that was a damn setup.

KING

Hell yeah, I was setting that ass up. I had gone three years without my baby. I still wasn't done getting all of the pussy that I missed out on while she was locked up. On top of that, I hadn't touched her in so long that a nigga was backed up and fiending. It wasn't just about the pussy, though; I missed my baby. I missed both of my babies. I wanted to be in my motherfucking house with my family, but I knew that I had fucked up royally without even knowing that I did! I felt stupid as hell for having a baby with Siren. I was just as much shocked and hurt about the shit as Kennedy was. I didn't feel like it was fair that I had to suffer the loss of my fucking family because of some shit that I did before Kennedy even came along. Siren had been a mistake since I put my dick in her all those years ago. However, Elijah was here. There was nothing I could do about him. But I couldn't expect Kennedy to accept him. I couldn't expect her to accept the fact that she had been so loyal to a nigga that she went to jail for, just to find out that I wasn't as loyal to her. But that was *one* motherfucking lie. That was the one thing that I'd ever kept from her that would hurt her. So I prayed that time would bring her back. In the meantime, I was going to try to bring her back with my words, actions... and this dick.

So by the time the third movie went off, Kennedy was a little buzzed and Kayla was sleep. As the credits started to roll, I looked over at Kennedy to see if she was about to give me the signal to leave, but she was on her phone. There was an insecure part of me that wondered who the fuck she was texting at one o'clock in the morning. It better had been Jada or Dre. But like I said, a small, doubtful part of me wondered if it was Glen. Kennedy had never given me a reason to mistrust her. I couldn't even picture her with another man, but there was no telling what she was feeling froggish enough to do after learning of my disloyalty. But I didn't even have one foot in the door and one foot out. Shit, *both* of my feet were out of the door, so I really wasn't in a position to question a damn thing. So, I took Kayla into my arms and carried her into her bedroom. She was already in her pajamas, so I was able to lay her down in her princess bed and cover her with her princess blanket. I kissed her on her forehead before leaving. Then I made my way back into our bedroom to try to seduce Kennedy into giving me the pussy that I know I didn't even deserve.

Once back inside of the room, I noticed that Kennedy was still in her phone. After the liquor had started to take effect, she had changed into something more comfortable than her jeans and tank top. Now she was in a t-shirt that barely covered her ass, so chunks of her cheeks were exposed and enticing me. I climbed into the bed, waiting for her to stop me at any moment, but she was now, not texting, but on Instagram. She wasn't paying me any attention. The liquor and Instagram had all of her attention. So I was able to sneak up on her, take the phone from her hand, toss it to the side and pull her under me.

"King, what are you doing? Stop it."

She was telling me to stop, but her fight had no bite. I didn't know whether it was because she was drunk or because she really didn't want me to stop and was just being stubborn. But, either way, I was taking advantage of either one.

"I'm so sorry," I told her as I kissed her forehead. And when she didn't push me away, I started to kiss down her face, her lips, her neck; I took my time kissing every inch of her that I missed while she had been away from me, and I told her over and over again, "I'm sorry, baby."

I knew that apologies weren't enough. Apologies weren't going to fix this. It fucked me up that I even had to apologize to her because I had never done anything to her that warranted an apology. I had always been the ideal nigga to her because she was always the ideal woman to me. It made me feel like less of a man to even be in this position to have to convince her to be with me.

Anyway, I was ready to fix the shit if it meant a million apologies, a million strokes, a million foreign cars or whatever the fuck she wanted.

I continued to trail her body with my lips and tongue, leaving a trail of evidence from where I had been to where I was going.

I swear it was crazy that I missed her so much that as soon as my nose was parallel with her pussy, I relaxed. I was home. I calmed because her scent did that to me. That's when I knew I was a dead man. If I didn't get this woman back, I would never be the same.

As soon as I licked it slowly, she hissed and her back arched, putting her pussy deeper into my mouth, and I welcomed that shit. But as I fucked her pussy with my mouth, I noticed that the body that I missed so much was not reacting to me in the same way. Kennedy would usually call my name, run her fingers through my hair, tell me how much she loved me, but even in her drunken state, she was only responding to me in whimpers and moans. There was no intimacy coming from her. It was like she was wondering why the fuck she was giving her body to me after what I had done to her while still trying to get the nut she hadn't bust since we split up. And even though I knew this, I kept going; I kept licking, sucking, and penetrating that pussy with my fingers as if it would bring her back to me. She was there, but she wasn't, and that was more of a fucked up feeling then her not being there at all.

CHAPTER 14

KENNEDY

His tongue felt so good in between my legs. But like I said before, I was no longer *that* Kennedy that gave him anything he wanted without question. This pussy that he was about to get was because I needed to get off, because my hormones were raging. I needed a release. It had nothing to do with him. So as he allowed me to orgasm inside of his mouth and brought his body on top of mine, I turned my head towards the bay window, looking out into the midnight sky. I was not about to kiss him and make fake love to him. I was not about to call his name and make him feel like a man because he was not at the moment. I just wanted to cum.

However, he kept his mouth next to my ear as his dick swam inside of me, as he put his body weight on mine and used his hands to hold my ass cheeks open, whispering over and over again, "I'm sorry, baby."

I even heard the sincerity in his voice, the desperation, the tears even. He wanted my forgiveness. He wanted my submission. He wanted the old Kennedy back. But it would take more than dick and "I'm sorry" to get her back.

"I missed this pussy so much, baby. I love you."

I wanted to respond, but he didn't deserve a response. He needed to know that hurting someone like this could ruin his life, the same way it ruined mine for three years, the same way that it was about to ruin his because it had taken me and his family away from him.

"Tell me you love me, Kennedy. Please tell me you love me. I need to hear it, baby."

I couldn't believe he would put me on the spot like this in the middle of the best orgasm I'd had in the last few weeks. He had my ankles on his shoulders now. He was holding on to my waist tightly, and his dick was driving inside of my pussy like a fucking maniac.

"Tell me you love me, Kennedy," he insisted.

"Oh God," I breathed. "Uhh!"

I knew that when I nudged him slightly, he would think that I was changing my mind about this sexual encounter, but that wasn't the case at all.

"What's wrong?" he asked.

I attempted to push him off of me, but he didn't budge. He moved his hands from my ass cheeks and used his elbows to level himself and look down at me curiously.

"I feel sick. I need to get up."

He was reluctant. I'm sure he thought I was lying. But in fact, I had forgotten that this baby, his baby, did not like alcohol.

"I'm too drunk," I lied. "I think I'm going to throw up."

Just as I had said the words, I could feel everything in my stomach swirling around like a violent tornado.

I moaned, "Uhhh," and King jumped up just in time for me to be able to roll out of bed, run to the bathroom and violently throw up into the toilet.

I felt King's hands on my back rubbing it soothingly as it seemed as if I would never stop vomiting.

Eventually, I began to dry heave, and that shit felt worse than throwing up. It was then that I knew that it was time for me to make an appointment at the clinic so that I can move on with my life.

After a few minutes, the nausea was gone, so I stood over the sink brushing my teeth and washing my face while avoiding King's eyes. I knew that he believed the excuse that I'd given him about drinking too much, but my conscience was still eating me up. I felt bad lying to him about the baby that he wanted me to have so badly, actually being in the bathroom with us.

As I threw my face towel into the dirty clothes basket, King asked, "Are you okay? Do you need some water or a BC powder?"

"I'm fine. I promise. You can go ahead and go. Don't worry about me."

King's face balled up. "Go? What you mean go?"

The old Kennedy would have never had the balls to tell King that he couldn't stay in his own damn house. However, he had fucked over the old Kennedy, so the new Kennedy told him, "Yes, go. You can't stay here. Just because we had sex doesn't mean that everything is okay and back to normal. I'm still hurt, I'm still mad, and I'm still not your woman."

I had never seen my man look so pitiful since I met him. That gangsta, beast mode, sexy ass swagger that I knew him to have was nowhere in his eyes when he looked at me, realizing that I was actually putting him out.

"You're never going to take me back are you?"

I didn't have an answer for him, so I didn't respond.

"This is something that I can never fix, isn't it?"

I still didn't have an answer for him. I didn't know how we could ever be the same.

Yet, as I stared at his massive, chocolate, muscular presence sitting on the tub, I couldn't imagine walking away from him and giving him to one of these bitches that would never love him the way that I had. I couldn't imagine another woman getting the fairytale hood love affair that I had experienced since I met him.

But I *could* imagine having all of that and having him throw it all away because he preferred being deceitful over being loyal.

My silence frustrated him. He ran his hand over his head and stood up. "Okay, Kennedy. I'll go."

I didn't stop him as he walked out of the bathroom. I simply closed the door to the bathroom because, even though I was strong enough to stand my ground, I was not strong enough to watch him leave.

KING

I felt like shit; I ain't gon' lie. I was walking out of my own damn house with blue balls, and it wasn't shit I could do about it because it was all my fault.

On my way out of the house, I stopped in Kayla's room and kissed her again. Then I headed out, running away from my own embarrassment. I couldn't believe that my life had turned into this all because of Siren. I had lost perfection, the most beautiful woman in the world, the most loving home, for the most disloyal slut that I had ever come across in my life. I had been in the game for years. I had run across some real savage ass niggas; niggas that would kill their own for a couple of bucks. But I had never met anyone as disloyal, calculating, and scheming as Siren.

I was a man used to getting my way. I was also a man that took his way if it wasn't given to me. I had been that way all of my life. What I wanted, I got. If there wasn't a way for me to take what I wanted, I made a way. I made my own lane. However, with Kennedy, I had no control. I couldn't use any of my gangsta ways to get her back into her heart. She wasn't giving it back to me. For the first time in my life, I would have to work hard, I would have to slave to even have the slim chance of getting what

I wanted. And what I wanted was my fucking family back like it was.

For the past couple of days, I didn't think luck was on my side at all, but as I climbed into my ride, my phone rang. When I saw who it was, I thanked God for a small streak of luck.

"Gustavo," I answered. "Please tell me you have good news for me."

Gustavo chuckled, and in his heavy, Spanish accent, said, "Yes, King, I have good news for you. You are lucky that you have been such a value to my organization. Otherwise, I wouldn't have gone through so much for you."

It was then my turn to chuckle. "I understand," I told him, "You know I wouldn't have called you for help unless I really needed it."

"Understood. Well, it's a go. Now handle this shit so that we all can continue to make money without fighting a hundred years in federal prison."

"Understood. I'm on it."

I hung up feeling more relieved than I had felt in a long time. If Kennedy wasn't taking me back, at least I was about to handle this shit with Siren and this bitch, Detective Sanchez. At least one part of my life was about to get back to normal. I would feel better trying to get Kennedy back if I wasn't looking over my shoulder waiting for the police to raid any or all of my spots and arrest me or any more members of my crew. Now that Gustavo had given me the word, I hoped that my plan worked out, that Siren and the detective would be gone, and Brooklyn would be free.

As I pulled out of my driveway, I called Meech. We had been so busy trying to handle this issue with Siren that he and I had no time to pay attention to any tension between us. We were both being man enough to look past my disloyalty to him in order to protect our families, our money, and to get rid of this snitch bitch Siren.

"What up, bruh?" he answered.

"I just got the call from Gustavo. It's a go."

Meech let out a heavy sigh immediately. "About motherfucking time. I'm so sick of that bitch."

"Well, you can get ghost for a few days if you want to. The shit will be handled soon. Maybe you should go out of town or something."

"Yeah, that sounds pretty good."

"Ah ight, bro. We'll chop it up in the morning. I'm on my way back to the telly."

Meech replied, "Damn, bruh. Kennedy still won't let you back in the crib?"

"Nah."

"Don't trip. She'll come around."

"I don't know about that," I sighed.

"Man, I can't see her throwing everything away over this. Just give her time to come around."

It fucked with me that Meech even had the heart to comfort me at a time like this. All of our worlds were upside down because of my decisions, because of my very few occurrences of disloyalty to them. Because he was still by my side, still my right hand, I would do anything to make sure this nigga was straight. Even if he chose not to fuck with me no more, I would always be there for him because he had shown me an inkling of forgiveness.

I just prayed that Kennedy would eventually come around and have the same forgiveness for a nigga.

MEECH

When I clicked over to the other line, all I heard was crying and kids yelling. This nigga's background sounded like a fucking zoo.

"Bruh, what the hell is going on over there?"

Dolla chuckled, but there was no humor in his laughter. It was actually sarcastic and a little pathetic. "Man, I have all the kids over here tonight."

"You mean Jada actually let the kids come over?"

"Yeah, man. You should have seen me trying to explain to Brittany and Brandon that the twins are their sister and brother."

"I bet Brittany tried to kill yo' ass like her mama did."

This time, his chuckle was actually humorous. "Yea. She tried to kill me with her damn eyes. She knows better than to disrespect me, but I can only imagine what the fuck she was thinking."

"That's crazy," I told him. "But, anyway, that was King on the other line. He said it's a go. I'm so fucking happy. I'm sick of looking at Siren's ass. Her motherfucking ass thinks she's slick. She think she got a chance. That bitch just don't know. I can't wait to get her out the crib. I got a replacement for her ass already."

Dolla asked, "Who? The yellow bone? London?"

"Yeah," I answered, as I looked towards London's mother's house. "I think shorty might have me pussy whipped."

Dolla started to laugh like that was the funniest joke he'd heard all year. "Damn, my nigga. Pussy whipped after one time? You only hit it once!"

"Well, let me stop frontin', trying to act like its just the pussy that got me like this. Real talk; I'm feeling shorty."

"Damn, bro," Dolla said. "Well, if you feeling her like that, then do you, bro."

"I plan to as soon as Siren get the fuck out of the way."

"Man," Dolla sighed long and hard. "I wonder if me and Jada will ever get back to that point again."

"You really done with her, bro?"

"It feel like it."

That shit was crazy to me. But hey, that's how men thought. We could run a woman through the ringer, stress her out, have a bitch so mad that she was in the nut house, and she will forgive us over and over again. But the moment we see her look at another nigga funny, our manhood is shot and we done.

"Damn, that's crazy. Y'all been together forever."

Dolla sighed again saying, "Right. We've all been together forever it seems like. The six of us have been at this for years. It's fucked up to see things changing the way that they are."

"Real talk."

"I can't be mad at all. I did the shit. I have to deal with the hand I dealt myself. It is what it is."

Just as I saw London's mother's front door open, I promised myself that I wouldn't deal myself another fucked up hand. I had no control over the outcome of me and Siren. I didn't know her shady ways before I chose to wife her. And even though I didn't know London well enough to know her shady ways, I planned to, to figure out if she had any so that she could be the real misses that I deserved. I had been content with Siren. The life we had was good. But now that I knew that she had been fronting on me the whole time, our entire relationship seemed like it was a fraud. All this time I thought that I had a real bitch. I thought that I had one of the best ones out here. And even though I had learned of her disloyalty before I met London, I was further convinced that there was something better out here the moment I met London. I actually was disappointed when me and Siren were over. I thought I would never have another rider like she was. I thought I would never have the connection that Kennedy and King had. I never thought that I would have the loyal woman that Dolla had. But I felt all of those things every time I was around London's stubborn ass.

I told Dolla, "Aye, bro. Let me holla at you later," just as London emerged from the front door and began stomping towards my car with her hands on her hips, which were swaying in a way that made me feel not so stupid for sleeping my big, yellow ass in front of her crib for the past few nights.

As soon as she leaned over into the passenger side window, her breasts spilling out of her green camisole, I told her, "Don't even start with me, London. I told you that I will be here every night to prove you wrong."

"Prove me wrong by taking me to your house, because that will tell me that she's actually gone."

"I can't do that yet."

"Then you need to leave."

"I don't think I do."

"I'm going to call the police on you."

"You aren't going to do that. You're not even cut like that. "

She sucked her teeth and folded her arms across her chest. She was frustrated because I was right. She wasn't some evil bitch that would call the police on a street nigga. Siren; that bitch would do some shit like that.

"What's wrong with me sitting out here to prove to you that you matter? If I was the type of dude that didn't care, you would be hurt. Now I'm sitting out here every night to show you how much I care, and it's still a problem, ma?

She had no answer for that. It looked like I had caught her off guard. So to further make a nigga look like a G, I said, "Now can you go back in the house? I'm tired, and I need get some rest."

Her mouth slightly fell open, and she fell further speechless. I starting rolling the window up, forcing her to step back. I smiled to myself as she stomped away from me and back towards her house. I watched her until she disappeared behind the front door, shaking my head.

I didn't give a fuck how much trouble London gave me; one way or another, I was going to get back in that pussy... and back in her heart.

Before turning up the music and firing up a blunt, I shot Siren a text message telling her that I would be out of town for the next few days overseeing a big drop in Tennessee. I knew that wouldn't go over too well. She had been on my ass since I had been spending every night out. She was trying to be calm about it because she knew she had to play her cards right to keep a roof over her head and a chance to get back with me. But what she didn't know was that nothing she did mattered. Her days were numbered.

CHAPTER 15

SIREN

"This motherfucker!" I growled as I banged my hand against the steering wheel.

Meech told me two days ago that he was going to be out of town. For two days, I had been ignoring my women's intuition. Something was telling me that who or whatever had him spending the night out for so many days was the same reason he was supposedly "out of town." I allowed my women's intuition to lead me to London's house. Lo and behold, I had spotted Meech's car sitting outside of London's house for two days straight.

Because my son was at home, I couldn't park outside and watch Meech all day and night like I wanted to. Meech had taken away certain amenities, like a nanny, once everything went down. Therefore, since it was the summer time, my days were filled with entertaining Elijah. I wanted so bad to sit in my car and camp out, watching what Meech and London were doing, but I could only drive past here and there when time permitted, like when Elijah was playing with friends, cousins, or when we were on our way somewhere.

As I drove past the block, I watched Meech's truck while trying to keep my eyes on the road at the same time.

I decided to call him to see what bullshit he would feed me next.

"Yo'. What's up, Siren?"

Siren. Not bae, not baby, but *Siren*. There was not one ounce of emotion in this man's voice for me. Even the small amount of affection that he had been showing me since I came back home was gone. I knew it was all because he was up under that bitch!

Calm down, Siren, I told myself. *Play your cards right, boo.*

I smiled so that the happiness could be in my voice as I said, "Hey. How are things going?"

"Things are going good. I should be home in like two days."

I rolled my eyes as I forced another smile and said, "Okay. Be careful."

"I will. I'll give you a call later on."

I ended the call and threw my phone in the passenger seat of my Porsche as I screamed out, "Arrrgh!"

I ran my fingers through my hair as anxiety crept in. I was losing Meech. I had already lost King and Jada, I had lost Dolla by default, and now I was about to lose Meech, and it was all my fault.

Angrily, I snatched my phone out of the passenger seat and dialed Jada's number. This bitch was supposed to do one thing. This bitch had one job; to make sure that I got my man back. Meech listened to the crew. If Jada and Dolla would have told him that he should stay with me, then that's what he would have done. He would not be at some low-rent house with some thot from the hood; he would be with me!

"What the fuck do you want, Siren?" Jada answered.

"Look, bitch, I'm not about to keep playing with you," I growled. "When I told you that I would keep you out of prison only if you did certain things, I was not fucking playing with you. You think that that detective is in my pocket because I don't help her in certain ways? I told you to make sure that Meech stays with me, and you haven't been doing that. Get it the fuck done, or end up in jail for attempted murder. This is not a fucking game. If this nigga leave me and I lose everything, I will make sure that you lose everything too."

Jada simply chuckled as she said, "You are crazy as hell."

"I am," I replied calmly. "I'm crazier than a motherfucker, and if anybody knows that, you do. But don't find out how crazy I can really be, Jada. I've been trying to be real calm about this shit, but you are making it impossible. *Do what the fuck I said, bitch.*"

Then I hung up.

KENNEDY

"That bitch is a psychopath," Jada said with a sarcastic laugh as she hung up the phone.

I sat next to Jada with bulging eyes. Jada had told me how crazy Siren had been since Jada saw her talking to that detective, but it was hard to actually believe. Siren had been nothing but a regular, down ass bitch all these years. Now, all of a sudden, she was this irrational, psycho, deceitful, bitch that was doing any and everything in her power to tear this crew apart. It seemed as if now she was trying to calm down and keep the peace because she didn't know who knew what, but losing Meech was something that was about to make her completely fucking lose it.

"I mean, what am I supposed to do about it?" Jada asked me. "What does she expect me to do? I can't make him be with her! Little does she know, that nigga don't want to be with her because he knows all the shit she's done. I hate that bitch."

"Just give it a minute, Jada," I told her. "King said that it will all be taken care of real soon. Nobody will have to deal with her anymore then."

Jada sucked her teeth. "Well, I wish he'd hurry up. I am so sick of her calling and threatening me. I'm not the type of bitch that takes threats lightly. I'm starting to look like a punk bitch because I have not gone over there and whooped her ass yet;

especially with all of this shit I'm going through with Dolla. I would love to go over there and take my aggressions out on her face."

I laughed. "I know. I hate the fact that I can't even confront her stupid ass, but if all goes well, she'll get what she deserves."

"Yea, but it will feel better if I had a hand in making her get what she deserved."

I laughed, agreeing, "I know, right? I would love to be there."

Just then, my phone vibrated, indicating that I had received a text message. As I assumed, it was King. He had called that morning telling me to get dressed because he had something to show me. I assumed that he was trying to buy his way back in, but there was no amount of money or no present expensive enough for him to purchase to fix this shit. However, I wanted to see what it was, so I got dressed in an Armani sundress, Giuseppe strappy sandals, and a ponytail. As I got dressed, Jada lay across my bed still fussing about Dolla and those twins until King called.

"That's King, girl. Let me go. He's outside."

"Well, call me, and let me know as soon as he shows you what your surprise is."

I smacked my lips, saying, "I will."

As I left out of the room, after grabbing my Kate Spade handbag, I was surprised at how nonchalant I was about this surprise King had. I wasn't sure whether it was the situation, the baby, or both that had my hormones on ten. I had no interest in him, what he had to say, his apologies, or his money.

When I walked outside, I couldn't resist how good King looked in his drop top, candy red, Maserati, picking at his full beard in the rearview mirror. King indeed looked like royalty as he sat in that foreign car. He was indeed the king of these streets. He was once the king of my heart, the ruler of my being. Now he was just a common man.

As I walked towards the car, and he got out of it to open the door for me, I didn't feel the usual effect that he had on me. I used to lose my breath in his presence. I used to be weak in the knees when he smiled at me. I used to be taken aback, and I felt like I was privileged to be with this man. Now he was just a man, a regular man, an ain't shit nigga that didn't deserve me, my loyalty, or my love.

What was even more strange was that I didn't even reach out to hug him as he opened the door and helped me inside of the car. I merely said, "Hey," softly and got comfortable in the passenger seat. I even looked at my phone and started to text my mom and dad to give myself something to do as we rode quietly down the highway towards the south side of the city. This was so strange for us. I usually would be so excited, asking him so many questions, trying to figure out what he had for his queen. However, I honestly didn't give a damn. I was merely taking the ride for shits and giggles.

His voice would pierce the silence with questions here and there about Kayla, if she needed anything, how the house staff was doing, if I needed anything, but I would answer so quietly and short that he would give up on forcing any further conversation.

About thirty minutes later, we pulled up in front of a storefront in the Bronzeville community on the south side of Chicago, the same neighborhood that his restaurant, Pearl's, was located. When he got out, I looked around the neighborhood curiously wondering what the hell we were doing there.

He took my door and opened it. Then he took my hand and helped me out and over the curb. We walked slowly, with him guiding me with his hand in my lower back towards a store that looked empty. When he used the key to open the front door, I started to smile on the inside, but I didn't let him see my happiness. I still wasn't completely sure what it was until we walked inside and I laid my eyes on the most gorgeous boutique I'd ever seen. It was painted in rich colors of milk chocolate and dark chocolate. I was standing on marble floors. The blinged out chandeliers and track lighting was amazing. Racks were full of high-end female clothing. There were bandage dresses, jumpsuits, blouses, jeans, anything a woman could think of, from the high-end labels to the affordable ones.

In the back of the store, there was a section for shoes. I noticed all of the name brand shoes that I have myself, including some that I had been dying to buy, but was too mad at King to ask for them. Then there were purses in a glass case; authentic Gucci, Louis Vuitton, Hermes, all of the labels that me and Jada slobbed over.

I looked up at King, who was watching me anxiously, seemingly like he was waiting for my response. There was some fear in his eyes, as if he didn't know what my response would be at all.

Though I knew already, to be a bitch, I asked, "What's this?"

"This is your boutique," he told me.

Like I said, on the inside, I was happy. As I looked around the store, I was amazed, though I was hurting. It reminded me of the store that Tricey had, and I couldn't wait for a grand opening.

Finally, I had something to do with my days, and I would be making my own money in the process. I had always been a hard worker when I was younger. My father made sure that I had a job and that I went to school. Ever since going to prison, I felt like I was a waste. I was doing nothing with my days. Even now that I was out of prison and was looking forward to starting school in the fall, I still felt like I wasn't doing anything extraordinary.

Now it looked like that might change.

When I didn't have a response yet, King went on to tell me, "You can decorate however you want. And I have a buyer that you can hook up with to get anything in here that you want. I just got a few things to get you started, and so that you can see the potential of the space. But you can change it. You can do anything you want."

It was like he was trying to convince me to be happy, to force the excitement on me. I was happy, but I wished that he was giving me this under different circumstances. I wished that he was giving this boutique to me because he felt like I deserved it, or because he wanted to, or because he loved me; not because he was trying to get me to forget that he had been so disloyal and dishonest.

"Thank you," I said giving him a weak smile.

He sighed sadly, as if he hoped my reaction was going to be so much more.

"Do you think this is going to fix everything?" I asked him.

It was as if he was disappointed that I was bringing this up. His shoulders shrunk and he avoided my eyes.

"I'm just asking, King. Do you think because you bought me this boutique that I'm supposed to forget that you kept something so important from me? That you allowed me to be friends with a woman that you had a sexual relationship with?

That you were so dishonest about things in your life that I possibly spent three years in jail because of your relationship with this bitch?"

King walked a few steps away from me and leaned against the counter by the cash register. "I didn't expect this to fix anything. This is something that you said you wanted. I had always planned to give it to you. Unfortunately, I wasn't able to surprise you until now. I know this isn't going to fix anything. Even if you never take me back, you're still the love of my life and the mother of my child, so I will always look out for you and give you whatever your heart desires."

That only pissed me off more. It made me even more depressed that we weren't together. This man had done something so great for me, and I wanted to be grateful. Yet, he had taken that opportunity from me. He had made it so that I couldn't even be happy when he did something so kind and loving. That shit was fucked up, and it just irritated me even more, despite the fact that this fetus was fucking giving me nausea that I couldn't control.

"Well, thank you. I appreciate it. But can we go? I'm not feeling well."

King was devastated. He tried to act hard and hide the sadness in his eyes, but I saw it. However, I was no longer available to comfort him. He had done this to himself.

DOLLA

"Brandon and Brittany want the new Jordans that are coming out tomorrow."

I didn't even look up from my phone as I stood in the doorway of my crib. I just told Jada dryly, "I got it."

I heard her suck her teeth, and that's when I knew that shit was about to hit the fan. Luckily, the nanny was upstairs with the twins and Brittany and Brandon had gone to Jada's car.

"Look," Jada told me. "If I had it to do myself, I wouldn't need to ask your ass. You got a lot of nerve treating me like this. I do one fucking thing, and you treat me like I'm the scum of the earth, but you been cheating on me for years and my stupid ass stayed right by your side, still loving your dumb ass."

I shrugged my shoulders, still looking through my phone as if I was really texting somebody, but I wasn't. "I didn't say shit, Jada."

"That's the problem! You haven't said shit to me since Marcus kidnapped me. You would think that you would, at least, give a fuck or ask me if I was okay-"

"You look okay to me," I said with a sarcastic chuckle that I knew was about to piss her off even more. "Shit, I bet you was real okay while you was gettin' some dick, wasn't you?"

Suddenly, she smacked my phone out of my hand. It shattered into pieces as soon as it hit the concrete. I was forced to look her in her eyes then.

"Fuck you, nigga! You've been fucking every piece of pussy in Chicago- shit, across the state- and you got the nerve to dismiss me because I finally did me? Fuck you, Dolla!"

I simply shrugged my shoulders. "Whatever, Jada. If that's how you feel, then why do you even give a fuck? Why you constantly arguin' with me and shit? If I been shitting on you all these years, then you got what you deserve, you got your freedom to go find you a nigga to treat you better than I did, right?"

That was the wrong thing to say. I knew it when I saw the sadness in her eyes. I knew that she wanted me to beg for her forgiveness, to beg for my family back, and I was prepared to do that at first. Shit, I *was* doing that for a few days after the twins had to come home. But when she played herself by being with that nigga, it showed me how much she really hated me. Yeah, my actions had pushed her into his arms, but she also looked happy to throw him in my face when I was standing in that club. That showed me just how much she really hated me. So even if we got back together, she would only be with me because she didn't want another bitch to have me, not because she was so fucking happy with me. I didn't even know if she had been truly happy to be with me or if she was just with me because she didn't want the next bitch to get what she had built over the years. Sometimes after you've been with somebody for so long, you don't know the fucking difference.

I was surprised when Jada sighed and was calm when she said, "You know what? You're right. I'll be buying Brittany and Brandon a cell phone tomorrow. You can call them if you need them or want to see them. There is no need for you to call me. Have a good night."

And now it was my turn to be sad. I guess seeing her turn up and be so angry with me made me feel like she actually still cared about a nigga. But when she walked away, I knew that her anger was starting to subside, and she was no longer giving a fuck. Watching her walk away showed me just how final this break up was. And when I didn't even have an urge to stop her or to apologize, I closed the door knowing that Jada and I would never be together again.

CHAPTER 16

SIREN

I couldn't believe that this motherfucker was still at this bitch's crib! I really didn't understand what they were doing because he wouldn't be there all day. He was just there at night. It was like he was living with her or something. But I also saw an older woman leaving out of the house every now and then, and she looked like an older version of London, so I knew it was her mother. If Meech was really fucking this girl like that, he would have put her up in a crib or bought her one of her own. Since he hadn't, I was really confused about what was going on, as I sat at the corner of her mother's block staring at Meech's Lexus truck. It was about twenty minutes after midnight. Meech had called me back like he said. He told me that he would be home the next day, Saturday, in the afternoon, and told me that his aunt was coming to pick up Elijah because she was taking all of the kids to a waterpark the next day. I was glad to get him dressed and out of the house because now I had the opportunity to stalk Meech as much as I wanted to.

However, there wasn't much action for me to watch. I was just sitting there watching his car so I figured that I might as well have gone to get me a drink since I had a Friday night to myself. I started the car, ready to go home, get dressed, and do me, just like Meech was doing him.

Maybe I can find me another baller so I don't have to deal with Meech and this bitch, I thought to myself as I pulled off.

But who the fuck was I kidding? I didn't give a fuck if I did meet another nigga with as much money as Meech; I was not letting him go simply because I was not about to let this bitch have my life.

I was so engulfed in my own thoughts that I didn't notice the blue and red lights behind me until the cars around me started to slow down. I also pulled over, giving the cop car room to go around us. However, when I pulled over, the cop car pulled over behind me is well.

"Urgh. I don't feel like dealing with this shit."

I immediately reached into my glove compartment for my driver's license and registration. However, when the police got to my driver's side door, I realized that this was not just some random ass traffic stop. I thought I had run a light or stop sign, too busy worrying about Meech and his bitch to pay attention, but clearly that was not the case when I was immediately ordered to get out of the vehicle.

I rolled my windows down. "Get out of the car for what? What did I do?"

The black officer ordered again, "Get out of the vehicle, ma'am."

There had been too many people dying in police custody for me to give a trigger-happy cop any problems, so I did what I was told, knowing that obviously this must have been a case of mistaken identity, or maybe they thought that since I was in a Porsche in that neighborhood that I was a nigga with some contraband in my car. I just knew that once they searched my car and ran my information, this shit would be over.

The officer led me to the backseat of the police car. Again, he didn't say a word as I asked him over and over again, "What are you stopping me for? Why did I have to get out of my vehicle? Are you searching my car? Do you have probable cause to search my vehicle?"

He simply slammed the door. That's when two more squad cars showed up.

What the fuck? I thought to myself.

I sat in the back of the squad car, placing a third phone call to Meech that he had yet to answer.

For all this nigga know I could be in some real trouble, and he's so busy up under this bitch that he don't give a fuck.

"Arrgh!!"

I sneered as I hung up the phone. Then, as I watched the officer search my vehicle, I figured that this had to have had something to do with Maria.

That bitch!

The last time I saw her, she thought I had set her up to get her killed, and she had been threatening me ever since. Of course, this was her doing. She was trying to push me around with police presence; typical, goofy police shit.

I called her next, but her phone went straight to voicemail.

You got to be fucking kidding me. I don't feel like dealing with this shit or this bitch.

I figured that this was what the fuck I deserved for even dealing with her snake ass. She was so obsessed with getting King, and now I wasn't helping her. Then she thought I tried to kill her, so of course she would put this much pressure on me. But little did she know, this shit wasn't going to work. I didn't have any product on me. I hadn't made a run for the crew in years. After King's precious Kennedy got locked up, the guys were very careful about what they allowed us to do because they didn't want to lose another one of us.

However, I was sadly mistaken. I *thought* there was no product in my car, but as I watched three officers dig inside of my car, one emerged with what I knew were bricks. Then another emerged from the back seat with more bricks. Then another emerged from the trunk with bricks and guns.

I gasped as my hands flew over my mouth! "Oh my God!"

I had no idea how all of that product got into my car. But hell, Maria was a slick ass bitch; she could have gotten someone to plant that shit in my car. Hell, her corrupt ass could have done it herself!

Tears filled my eyes. I couldn't believe this shit!

Even though I was in the back seat of the police car and the windows were rolled up, I began to scream as I banged on the window, "Those aren't mine! I don't know how that shit got there!"

I started to punch the windows and kick the back seat in anger. I was so fucking pissed! I was so wrapped in getting Meech back that I wasn't even paying attention to this bitch set me up!

One of the officers rushed towards the door and snatched it open.

"Calm the fuck down!" he shouted.

"That shit isn't mine," I screamed. "That bitch set me up! She set me up! I know she did! That bitch set me up!"

The officer chuckled and shook his head, patronizing me as he said, "Of course, it's not yours."

"I'm serious! I need to speak to Detective Sanchez. Detective Maria Sanchez!"

The officer froze and stared down at me with curled eyebrows. His stare was judgmental, as if he was trying to figure me out or some shit.

His silence was pissing me off, so I snapped. "What?!"

"You want to talk to Detective Maria Sanchez?"

"Yes! Damn!"

"You can't speak to Detective Maria Sanchez. She was killed in a home invasion this morning."

MEECH

I sat in one of the crew's trap cars across the street in a BP gas station, watching as the police pulled brick after brick out of Siren's Porsche. She had been blowing my phone up, which I expected, but I ignored that shit. Watching our plan begin to unfold, I felt a small bit of relief. But Siren had been such a sneaky ass bitch that she had been able to get away with a lot of bullshit. In the back of my mind, I wondered if she would be able to get out of this too. But King and Gustavo had so much pull in the police department and the governor's office that I wanted to believe that there was no way that she would get out of this shit.

As I put the car in drive, I shot King a text message, letting him know that the first part of our plan was in motion. Then I headed back over to London's mother's house. Yea, my goofy ass had still been camping out at her crib every night. But, honestly, it was better than sleeping under the same roof as Siren.

I chuckled as I pulled onto her block and saw her in the driveway when I pulled up. I knew she was about to curse me out, and by now, the shit turned me on.

I parked the trap car behind my truck and then sent one of the guys a text message, telling them to get a ride to come pick it up. I felt a couple of pounds lighter as I got out of the car, realizing that that bitch wasn't in my house no more. I would feel a hell of a lot better once everything was done, Siren was gone for good, and my cousin, Brooklyn, was back at the crib.

"Go home, Demetrius," I heard London's voice say.

I looked up and saw her standing next to her truck. She looked like she had been out. She was dressed in a beautiful cream bandage dress, burnt orange heels, and her dreads had been styled in an updo.

Shit, a nigga had to exhale as I lay eyes on her. I felt like I was in a soft ass movie or some shit. She had me feeling like a chump. But if I was going to be a chump for anybody, London was the girl to do it with.

"Did you just call me by my government name?" I asked her.

She ignored the way that I looked her body up and down. She was so high-yellow that I could see every inch of her in the darkness of the midnight sky. She folded her arms across titties that I wanted to be in my mouth so fucking bad. Then she put all of her weight on one leg, causing that hip to pop out. I wondered if she was doing this shit to prove a point or turn me on.

"This shit is stupid. You don't have to keep sleeping out here every night. It's been a couple of days."

"So do you get the point?" I asked. "Because if you don't, I'm getting in the car and going to sleep."

Her eyes rolled into the back of her head. "You are so crazy."

"For you, I told you."

"Meech-"

I saw her weakness. Her stubbornness was starting to go away as I walked towards her and told her, "Let me come in and talk to you. Then I'll go. I promise."

"I'm not letting you in, Meech."

"If I can't come in, then come home with me."

That threw her off. Her stubbornness was completely gone then and was replaced with shock.

As soon as I got word from my housekeeper that Siren had left out that evening, I knew that she wouldn't be returning. We all knew that that night, Siren was being tailed, would be stopped by the police, searched and arrested. So, I had the housekeeper clean my house from top to bottom, getting rid of anything that was related to Siren. Every picture, every toiletry, and she even cleaned out Siren's room, getting rid of everything in there and the closet. This invitation to London was not for her to come live with me. We were still going to take it as slow as we had been before. But if she said yes, she could come, then I was going to show her just how much I missed her.

I smiled at her confusion and reiterated. "You heard me. Come home with me."

LONDON

Shit, he had me at hello. Well, not really, but he had me the night that he slept outside of my house for the first time. But I couldn't give in just then because it was obvious that she still lived with him. Even though he had gone to great lengths to show me that he cared, he had yet to show me that she was gone... Until now.

Hearing him ask me to come to his house was all that I needed to hear. I was game. It was kind of embarrassing the way that I just gave in, but I figured that I had given the man enough trouble. Not only had he shown me that he cared about me and that I mattered to him, but the nigga deserved some pussy when he left that truck in my driveway!

I tried to hesitate a bit, but I could see in the small smirk on his face that he knew my hesitance was full of shit, so I just gave up and walked towards him. As soon as we were within arms reach, he wrapped his arms around me, and I just fell into his embrace. I missed him so much. I was so tired of fighting, and I was so happy that I could finally just let go and enjoy him. I didn't know Meech like that. Just because this chick was gone, I didn't know their history, I didn't know what would happen the next day, and I didn't even know what would happen with me and Meech, but what I *did* know was that that night, I was going to thank him for going out of his way to show me that he cared; I was going to show him in *so many* ways.

He took me by the hand and led me towards his truck. He opened the passenger side door, guided me in, and then rushed over to the driver's side. As soon as he got in, I grabbed his face and started to kiss him. I had been fantasizing about his tongue in my mouth for so long. My pussy leaked as he sucked my mouth and I moaned into his.

As we kissed, he told me, "I missed you, ma."

The words he spoke into my mouth made my pussy so wet for him that I couldn't even wait to get to his house.

"I missed you too," I moaned as I leaned over, pushing him back into his seat. Then I straddled him. I reached down between the seat and the door and pushed a button, thinking that I would let his seat back, but the seat actually began to rise.

We both giggled.

"The one next to that button," Meech directed me as his mouth found my neck and he started to lick and suck it.

I finally found the right button and his seat went back. His hands hurriedly pushed my dress up, and I lifted up slightly so that he could get that dick out of his jeans. I didn't give a fuck if we were in the street under the street lights. I didn't give a fuck if we were right in front of my mother's house. I wanted this man so fucking bad. I had played hard to get for long enough. I needed that dick. I wanted that dick more than I wanted my next breath.

That might be extreme, but you would feel the same if you ever had the opportunity to be on top of a man like Meech.

As soon as his dick was in my sight, I pushed my panties to the side, rested on my tip toes, braced myself on his armrests and slid down on it slowly.

"Oh my God," left my throat in a hungry moan.

Meech grabbed my ass cheeks, squeezing them, and spreading them apart, causing his length and width to bury itself inside of my pussy.

"Fuck, baby. I missed this pussy," he groaned as his mouth found mine. Then he spoke into my mouth as he started to passionately kiss me, saying, "I missed you."

It felt like he'd missed me too. He was definitely showing me how much he missed me with this dick. But besides the sex, I felt how much he missed me as he held me. He grabbed my ass tight and pressed against my chest so tightly, as if he never wanted to let go.

I dared not think that this man could be my future. I was scared to even think that far. He hadn't been around for that long, and let's not forget all of the drama that I had had since I met him. But there was something about his touch, there was something about the way he looked at me, there was something about the way his dick felt like it belonged inside of me, that made me want to take the chance to see if we had a future beyond the good times, the laughs, and the good sex.

"Shit!" I gasped as Meech held on to my waist and started to push each one of his many inches all the way inside of me, forcing me to bounce on top of his dick. I reached up, bracing myself on the roof, and I rode his dick with just as much aggression as he was forcing me to. He bit his lips as his eyes rolled back in his head and he leaned back against the headrest.

"Fuck!" I squealed. "This dick feels so *fucking good,* Meech! I missed this dick! I missed you!"

The whole fucking block probably heard me, but I didn't give a fuck. This dick was so good that everybody needed to know, even my mama.

CHAPTER 17

KENNEDY

"You expect this to make me feel better, King?"

"It don't?"

I chuckled sarcastically and shook my head. "First, you expect a boutique to fix this, and now, just because Siren is gone, I'm supposed to forgive and forget?"

I sucked my teeth and shook my head in disgust. "Sure wish you had this type of pull when I was facing my time."

My eyes cut at King and his chest sank. "Really?"

That was mean, and I knew it. If King had this type of pull back then – shit, if he had the relationship with Gustavo then that he did now- I knew that he would have made sure that I would have never had to spend one night in jail. But I refused to take back what I had said, so I ignored King's hurt and focused on folding the skinny jeans.

King looked just as helpless as he did a week ago when he had surprised me with the boutique. Luckily, since then, I'd been managing the opening of the boutique to take my mind off of my pregnancy and King. Jada and I had spent a lot of time promoting the grand opening on Instagram, Facebook, and Twitter. Since the both of us had nothing to do prior to, the boutique was now our new baby. It was also our way to get our minds off our fucked relationships. We were putting all of our energies into it. I planned on opening it in two months and having a huge grand opening. It felt so good to finally be back to the old me; the ambitious and driven Kennedy, the independent Kennedy. Even though King had given me this boutique, I planned on making it such a success that I would eventually buy King out. I wanted this to be truly *my* store so that I could start building my own empire.

Even though I was putting all of my energy into the boutique, King was putting all of his energy into me, especially now that Siren was locked up. When I found out that she had been arrested, I did feel a bit of relief. It was only fair that she got to feel the pain that I felt while being away from my man, my child, my family, and my crew. However, she would get it back ten times worse because, from what King was telling me, she would never see the light of day again. I know that he had only spared her life because she was Elijah's mother. And that small bit of consideration pissed me off. That bitch did not deserve any consideration whatsoever, so I was not as pleased as he would have thought I would be. However, it did show me why I had been so committed and loyal to him previously. When it came to those close to him, when it came to family, he was loyal enough to spare the rod. I also knew that for a money hungry, attention seeking, obsessive bitch like Siren, being locked up was just the same as death.

King sighed as he leaned against the back door office of the store. I knew that he was frustrated. For a week, he had been professing his love, convincing me of how sorry he was, and literally begging to be back with me. But all that I could think of was how I had sacrificed three years of my life, three years away from my daughter, for him and the crew, and two of the members of that crew were playing the fuck out of me the whole time.

I looked at King and saw my life, I saw my love, and I saw my soul. I imagined divorcing him, and the shit made me sick to my stomach. But he had done some things that I just couldn't imagine myself forgiving. I hoped that the pregnancy was what was making me despise him this much. But in a matter of hours, the pregnancy would be taken care of.

"Kennedy, I can't continue to live without you. I waited three years for you. I waited and imagined being back with you every single day that you were gone. I never looked at another woman. Never touched another woman. Never had any interest in any woman, except you. And now that you are out, I cannot believe that I still don't have you."

His words had moved me. I started to shift through a rack of straight leg jeans as I forced back the feeling of submission. "I can understand all of that. Do you realize that I lay in that bed every night feeling the same way? I never imagined getting out of prison and still not being with you."

"Then why not be with me?"

"Because you fucking hid all of this from me! Do you realize that she was probably so eager to set you up because you fucked her and, not only married somebody, but nearly married two people in her face? I'm a woman, King. I know how it feels to sleep with somebody and have them choose someone else over me! That shit don't feel good!"

"I didn't play with her feelings. I was always straight up with her!"

"But were you always straight up with me? Just because I never asked you have you ever fucked with her, you should have volunteered that information to me! Do you know how stupid I feel knowing that I hung out with this girl for years, that I was ride or die for this girl for years, that she was part of the reason why I took that time, and the whole time, she was the reason why I was in jail in the first place? Every time I look at you, I'm reminded of that. Every time I see your face, I am reminded how naive I was, how gullible I was to believe that everybody around me was so loyal, so loving, so committed to me that I would give away three years of my life for them. I cannot take you back, wake up to you every day, and be reminded of that every fucking day."

King looked intently into my eyes as he told me, "Please let me show you that the time you spent in prison was not in vain. Please let me show you that I am the loyal man that you thought I was before you came home. I am still the same man that you made that sacrifice for, Kennedy."

I wanted to believe that. I wanted to wholeheartedly feel that all of that was true so that I could have my picture perfect family back. I liked being naive. I liked being gullible. It didn't hurt. Sometimes some things are better left unsaid. I could imagine how much better my life would have been if I had never heard King say the words that tore us apart.

However, I didn't say any of that to him. I was tired of repeating myself. There was nothing that could fix this but time. King needed to pray and ask God to put forgiveness in my heart because right now it was not there. Lucky for me, his phone vibrated, causing him to take his attention away from me and put it on the text message that he was now reading.

Once he was done, he returned the phone to his pocket and reluctantly said to me, "I have to go take care of this shit at the county. Please just think about what I said. I know it will take some time, so I'll stop pressuring you."

I sighed and simply nodded. As he walked by me, he grabbed the side of my face and kissed my forehead.

SIREN

A week later, I was still sitting in the county jail. I was arrested very early on a Saturday morning. Once I was told that Maria had been killed, all kinds of thoughts ran through my mind. Though she was dead, I still thought that she could have been behind this until I was booked, allowed a phone call and no one answered my calls; not King, Kennedy or Dolla, and definitely not Jada or Meech.

There was only one conclusion to come to; Jada had obviously run her mouth, and the crew had set me up. I assumed that was why Maria was killed, and I was being set up. What I didn't know was why King had allowed me to live. Jada had told him something or everything, so why he had let me live was a mystery.

King had all types of resources, especially because of his relationship with Gustavo. There was no telling where their connections lie or how deep they went. I learned that that was obviously the case when on that Monday, I was told that I was being charged with federal offenses. I was told that this was a federal case because someone else facing federal charges had snitched and told that I was a major drug supplier in Chicago. The shit sounded absolutely ridiculous to me, but I had obviously been set up perfectly. No matter what the public defender that I was given argued, I wasn't granted a bail. It was as if the prosecutor was out to get me and the public defender left me out there to be slaughtered. I was a young mother with no record, and they had no probable cause to search my vehicle, as far as me and my attorney felt. However, the judge was on the prosecutor's side, agreed to each of her arguments and objections, and denied me bail. I would have to sit in jail while I faced multiple felony charges that were going to definitely land me in the Feds for many years because I had an inexperienced public defender since I didn't have any money to hire a lawyer. The charges I was facing then held twenty to thirty-five years minimum. I wouldn't even see Elijah graduate from elementary school. If I was able to see him graduate from high school, it would be a blessing.

I had even offered the prosecutors any and all evidence that they wanted on King and his organization. In the past, I was working with Maria out of pettiness, because King didn't want me. Now it was because I wanted the opportunity to at least see my son again.

Then, two days ago, the prosecutor visited me, letting me know that there had been evidence found in the home invasion of Detective Maria Sanchez. Prints at the scene belonged to me, along with a gun found near her home with my fingerprints. It was obvious that this evidence had been planted, but the prosecutor didn't give a fuck about any of that. She wouldn't listen to anything I was saying, which made me feel like, hell, she was in on it too. No matter what I said, she was charging me with federal drug and murder charges, which meant that I was never getting out of prison.

I had been set the fuck up, and there was nothing I could do about it. I actually felt like I deserved it, after everything I had done. Previously, all of my anger was towards King, and I never honestly wanted to see Kennedy in prison. I had feared that sending an innocent girl to prison would eventually come back on me, and it had. I was fighting so blindly to keep my relationship with Meech that I was gullible, not realizing that the entire crew was out to get me. Now my life was actually really being taken away from me. I thought Meech leaving me would be it. But this; this really was it.

This set up had truly taken my life away. I had might as well had been dead. I felt like I was dying and tried everything I could to get out of it. But there was nothing I could do. King was a genius. This set up was in typical King fashion, executed perfectly and left me just as I was sure they wanted me; tortured, dying on the inside and wishing for death.

KING

Later that afternoon, me, Meech and Dolla went up to the county. It was time that Siren knew exactly what her fate was.

The governor and Gustavo did a lot of business together. Gustavo made contributions to the governor's campaign in order to make sure that the Fed's stayed away from his organization. Once Gustavo called the governor and asked for this favor on behalf of one of his most loyal and most successful suppliers, the governor called a prosecutor at the county and told her to make sure that Siren would spend the rest of her life in prison. Then my connections in the police department helped plant the evidence in Maria's house after I shot that bitch in the back of the head while she was sleeping. The prosecutor was given instructions to make sure that that case against Siren stuck as well.

I knew that Siren deserved nothing but a brutal death. Siren deserved for me to strip her naked and torture her until I got tired, then set her on fire, douse her with water right before she died, and then set her on fire again. However, she was the mother of my child. I couldn't stomach doing something so brutal to her. However, this plan that I had concocted was actually way worse than death. It was worse than her being in the grave because she would live every day wishing that she was dead. What's worse, she would have to live every day knowing that the one person that she hated the most and the one person that she envied the most would be raising her son. She fought so hard to have a certain position that she would now never have with anyone that she wanted it with; all of that would kill her and make every breath that she took torturous.

When we walked into the visitation room, she looked relieved to see Meech but confused when she noticed me and Dolla behind him. She stayed seated as we walked toward her, but her eyes were full of questions and concern.

We all sat down, but I was the one that sat directly across from her. She saw the storm in my eyes and looked at Meech with eyes that were begging for help, for him to say something, but he had no words for her.

I had all the words to say. "You already know what it is, I'm sure, so let's get straight to the point. You'll never get out of here. You have two choices; you can fight this case and still end up with life in prison, or, when the prosecutor offers you thirty years tomorrow, you take it."

She tried to act like that didn't faze her, but I saw right through that shit. Even though she had only spent a week in prison, it already looked like she had aged damn near five years. The glitz and glam was gone. She had already lost so much weight. She could sit across from me like she wasn't scared but I knew that she was.

"If it wasn't for Elijah, I would have killed your ass, like I snuck through Maria's window and killed her motherfuckin' ass, but since you're the mother of my child, I'm allowing you to at least still live... physically."

As soon as I said that, Siren's eyes closed tightly and then looked towards Meech, who gave her a condescending look. He told me that he had no words for her after she was gone, and he was living up to his word. He didn't have shit to say to her.

"Yeah, I know that's my child, and I know that you put Kennedy in prison. So now you have to sit here while me and Kennedy raise your son."

As soon as I said the last few words, Siren jumped over the table and started to attack me.

"I HATE YOU!!"

She was punching my face and scratching at my eyes. The entire visitation room went up! Some people were screaming and others were moving the fuck out of the way while guards charged towards the table. Guards snatched Siren up, but she held on to my top fro and neck tightly. I didn't touch her because I knew the way that I was smiling at her was hurting her worse than any blow to the face that I could give her.

Eventually, the guards were able to pry her hands away from me, and she was drug out of the visitation room screaming, "I hate you, King! Die, nigga! Fuck you!"

JADA

Since picking up the kids from Dolla's house a week ago, my attitude had changed from anger and sadness to the realization that my relationship was over and probably for a good reason. I had forgiven Dolla over and over again to the point that he didn't respect me. He had lost all admiration for me, for the woman that he knew I was. Anyone who knew me and truly respected me knew that I was not that type of bitch. Anyone else would not have been surprised to find me with Marcus. Even though Marcus ended up being a huge mistake, going out with him was not my fault. Dolla had no right to judge me for that. He had cheated on me so many times that I should have at least had five dicks on reserve.

The fact that he was judging me for that one mistake let me know that he had not put me on the same pedestal that I had put him on. He obviously didn't love me as much. Obviously, his loyalty did not run as deep. It made me feel sick to the stomach to know that I had been so ride or die, so loyal, so committed and so willing to risk anything for someone who was not willing to do the same. He had not been willing to sacrifice one damn thing. Not only was he not willing to sacrifice staying away from these bitches, but he also wasn't willing to sacrifice his manhood or his ego to show me one ounce of sympathy or compassion.

That was *not* love.

"So you're really done?" my mother asked me.

I was sitting at my mother's house on a Friday afternoon. The summer was in full swing. It was at least eighty degrees at night. We were sitting on her back patio in her house in Calumet City, Illinois. My children were in the yard playing in the pool with some of their cousins.

"Yes, mama, I am really done," I sighed.

My mother shook her head sadly as she said, "I just can't believe it. After all you've been through, after as strong as you've been, you're going to just walk away from your stability?"

Of course, because she was my mother, I hadn't told her *everything* that I had gone through with Dolla over the last eight years. She didn't know about every time he cheated, and she definitely didn't know about Marcus kidnapping me and how Dolla treated me afterward. But she did know about some of the random women that called my phone and the ones that I caught Dolla up with here and there. Yet, to an old school woman like my mother, cheating was not a reason to leave a man that took care of the household. The only reason that she was not with her husband was because he had died from a heart attack. Yet, I remembered my stepfather cheating here and there, and my mother never batted an eye. She also never had to work a nine-to-five or ask her husband twice for anything that she wanted.

As I thought about that, I questioned whether my decision to walk away from Dolla was legit. I sat there looking at my kids, realizing that I would have to take care of them. Sure, their father would take care of them financially. But he would not take care of me. The respect and love that King had for Kennedy was not present in Dolla's heart for me, so I couldn't bank on him taking care of me even though we were no longer together. The lifestyle that I was used to, I would have to maintain on my own. I had never had an issue with getting out there and hustling, but as a single mother of two, I could no longer risk the repercussions of being in the streets just for a dollar. I would have to walk a straight and narrow line in order to remain free for my kids, which meant that I could no longer get the fast money that I was used to.

"All right, mama. I ain't gon' lie; it scares the hell out of me to know that I won't have my comfort zone anymore. I've never been to college. I don't have any work experience, and I can't be out here in the streets like Dolla."

"Exactly, baby. Some things you might have to turn a blind eye to just to secure the future of you and your kids. It doesn't make you stupid; it makes you smart."

CHAPTER 18

KENNEDY

The next morning, I was riding to my appointment with butterflies in my stomach. I was alone. I didn't have the courage to tell Jada about it, so I was doing this on my own. Jada thought that I was simply going to a doctor's appointment, and I had convinced her that I didn't need her to come with me.

When my phone rang, and I glanced at the Caller ID, I cringed when I saw the name on the display. As I approached a stop sign, I quickly answered through the Bentley's Bluetooth.

"Hey, King."

Then I held my breath, hoping that he hadn't sensed something and was calling to stop me. He was a man of many connections, and it seemed like he always found out everything.

"You got a minute?" he asked me.

It sounded like he didn't know what I was doing, but I still rolled my eyes as I hit the gas and continued in my direction. I was relieved that he wasn't on to me, but I was irritated because it sounded like he was about to start the same "I'm sorry" and "Will you take me back?" conversation that he had been repeating for a week straight.

"Yeah. What's up?'

"Today is Elijah's birthday. I plan on going to the birthday party that Meech is having for him at his crib. I plan on telling him that I'm his real father. I'd really like you to be there."

Once again there was a timidness and fear in King that I wasn't used to. Before I left him, I only heard this fear in his voice when we talked about me serving my time. I felt sorry for him. I knew that talking to Elijah would be a lot for him, but I had to stop looking out for King and start looking out for myself.

"I don't think so, King. I'm not really ready for that."

There was some hesitation before he said, "Okay. I understand."

I was prepared to explain myself, but then the line went dead, and that's when I realized that King had hung up the phone. I didn't have time to focus on that conversation or King's response, though. I was pulling up in front of the Family Planning Associates building. There were protesters outside with life-sized pictures of babies with quotes about how abortion is a sin. Yet, I pulled into the parking lot unbothered by any of that. The incidents that had occurred over the past couple of weeks had shown me that I had been more loyal to others than I had been to myself. I could no longer make decisions that would greatly affect my life based on King. Now that I was about to start school, and I had my own business, I felt like the old Kennedy. I was excited about what my future held, even if it did not include King as my husband. The excitement in my heart, despite the hurt, made me realize that my life did not have to revolve around King for it to be a happy and good life.

As I got out of my car, a staff member of Family Planning Associates quickly approached my car. She smiled at me saying, "Good morning. We have a lot of protesters out this morning. I'm here to escort you in. Just ignore them and don't respond to them."

I nodded my head as she locked her arm in mine and walked me through the parking lot and across the street, past the protesters, who yelled at me about Jesus and quoted bible scriptures, and into the waiting room full of women.

I registered for my appointment and paid for the procedure. I had to have waited at least an hour before my name was called to the back, but it only felt like a few minutes because I was consumed with both good and bad thoughts. Being at that clinic made me feel like my life was making a drastic change. I had never defied or lied to King. But keeping his baby from him and aborting it behind his back was just as much of a dirty move for me, as him keeping his relationship with Siren. I wondered was

I doing it to get him back. I knew that I was doing it for me, though.

However, now there was no way that we could ever be a couple again because I would never lie to his face or be a hypocrite. After this procedure was done, I had to let go of him and let go of the hurt that his relationship with Siren had caused me. I was now just as much of a bad person that King was.

"Kennedy Carter."

I jumped as my name was called, realizing that I could possibly be outted. But then I realized that I had driven all the way to Michigan for this procedure for this very reason. I still rushed to the back towards the nurse that held a smiling, pleasing face. She walked me towards the back, making me feel at ease, even though I had never undergone this procedure before. I was told to undress and was given an ultrasound.

I was then told to wait in another smaller waiting room. There were other women in the room waiting along with me in patient gowns. Only one other woman looked as stoic as I did; like me, it looked like she just wanted to get this shit over with. The other three were chatting it up like this was an ordinary day, like they were kicking it at the bar or something. They talked about their babies' daddies. One said how she didn't want her baby because her baby's daddy had a wife with three kids already. The other chick said that her baby's daddy didn't want the baby because he didn't know if it was his or her husband's, and one of them didn't even know who her baby daddy was, so that's why she was doing it. I shook my head discreetly, their ratchetness making this more difficult for me. They were irritating me when I was already irritated. I just wanted to get this over with, so I could go back to my boutique and continue my life like none of this ever happened, including me finding out who Elijah's father really was.

"Kennedy Carter."

I jumped out of my seat, so happy that my name had finally been called. I followed the nurse into a cold examination room. I was instructed to lay on the hard table that reminded me of the cot I slept on in prison. Then a masked man came into the room, his eyes smiling at me. He approached me and placed a warm and soothing hand on my arm.

"I'm the anesthesiologist," he told me. "I'm going to put you to sleep, okay?"

I closed my eyes as he started to prepare the liquid that would put me to sleep for a little while. I expected to feel some sadness, I expected to feel some type of reluctance, but when I didn't, I knew that what I was doing was right.

With a deep breath, I looked into the eyes of the anesthesiologist and said, "Okay."

JADA

When I arrived at Meech's house for Elijah's birthday party, I was so pissed and irritated when I saw Dolla's car. I knew that he would be there, but I hoped that something would have happened to prevent him from coming; a car accident, the flu, food poisoning, something! I knew that he would have those fucking twins with him, and it made me feel like an idiot that I was about to be at a party with the crew, our friends, and our children, and everybody would be looking at these twins like, "Where the fuck did they come from?" The way that Dolla had played me would be obvious to everybody, and it would be so fucking embarrassing!

"Come on, y'all. Let's go," I told Brittany and Brandon reluctantly.

They literally ran out of the car because they knew that they were going to a party and were super excited. They had a right to be. Because the crew had so much money, our parties were lavish, including our kids' parties. And since it was the summertime, Meech had already told me that the pool party would include barbecue, games, ponies for the girls to ride, bumper cars for the boys to ride in the field next to Meech's house, and a lot more.

They were excited, but I was reluctant as we walked up to Meech's front door. The door was open, so I walked in with my head held as high as possible. I looked good on the outside, of course. I was dressed from head to toe in the finest labels, my hair was laid, and my face was beat for the gods, but on the inside, I felt pathetic and just wanted to go lie in bed with the covers over my head and dodge this party altogether.

Once inside of the house, I heard all of the voices that I recognized inside of the kitchen. The kids ran in that direction, and I solemnly followed. Inside of the kitchen was Meech, a light- skinned girl with dreads that I knew was London because he had sent me pictures of her, bragging that she was "the one," Dolla, and the chef that was barbecuing for the party. To my surprise, I did not see the twins or hear their cries, so I was relieved.

I guess Dollar does have some compassion in his heart, I thought.

The kids excitedly spoke to everyone in the kitchen, especially their dad, and then Meech told them that Elijah was waiting for them in the pool. Even though the party hadn't started, Elijah couldn't wait so he had already started to party.

"You guys be careful. No running around the pool," I told the kids.

They shot over their shoulders, "Okay, mom," and then ran out of the patio door in the kitchen.

Meech then started to look between me and Dolla. I knew he was expecting it to be some drama, but I was tired of the drama, so I looked at London, saying, "Hey. I'm Jada. Nice to finally meet you."

As London smiled, I reached out to hug her slightly. Meech was right; she was so beautiful. I just hoped that her outside appearance matched her inside, for Meech's sake. He had been spending a lot of time with her since Siren went away. He had even introduced her to Elijah. They weren't technically in a committed relationship yet, but I knew the time was coming soon because all they were missing was the title at this point.

Meech looked at London and said, "Baby, let me talk to them for a few minutes in private."

"Okay. I want to go change into my swimsuit anyway," London told him.

"Aye," Meech quickly told her. "It better be something that covers all that ass up. I don't want these niggas looking at you."

She simply giggled as she left out of the kitchen, and I looked at Meech as if I couldn't believe the man standing before me. He definitely was a new, happier man, and I was so happy for him.

Once we heard London going up the stairs, Meech told us, "Siren took the deal. She'll be serving thirty years."

A sigh of relief escaped all of us. We were relieved that Siren was officially out of our way. The crew was still in good standing, still free to make the money and rule the streets like we had always been, now that Siren and Detective Sanchez were out of the picture for good. Of course, there would be new enemies coming to try to take our empire down, but we would take care of them just like we had taken care of this.

Just then, we heard others coming through the front door. It sounded like Kennedy and King, so Meech immediately left the kitchen to greet them, and I was about to follow when Dolla stopped me.

"Aye, Jada, hold up."

I looked at him and immediately got defensive. I was expecting for him to start some more shit with me. I had been trying to avoid him as much as possible because of this; because of the intense amount of tension that was between us.

But I was surprised when he said, "Look, I just wanted to say that I'm sorry for the way I've been treating you. You were right. What you did was no comparison to all of the things I've done to you over the years. You were so ride or die, and I totally took advantage of that. I didn't plan for the twins to be here and when they got here, I knew that telling you would be the worst thing I could ever do to you. That's why I didn't. But I was forced to, and they're here now. And we are going to have to be a family, whether me and you are together or not. I know it's going to take you a long time to accept them, but I just hope that you can eventually so that we can be cordial around our kids."

My usually snappy attitude with Dolla was scared to show up. Here he was being the responsible adult, and I wasn't used to that shit. I was floored and didn't know how to take this from him.

I nodded my head in agreement. "You're right. I've been so hurt that I've been irrational. But I promise that I'll try to be as cordial as I can. I don't know how easy it will be. I know I've been clowning, but I'm hurt. It's obvious that our relationship is really over, and it just hurts, you know?"

I don't know what I wanted him to say. Like, in the back of my mind, I wanted him to say that it wasn't over, that he would do everything in his power to fix our relationship. I wanted him to say that he loved me so much and would die without me. But I knew that even if he did say all of that, it wouldn't fix anything, I would still be hurting and still be this angry, bitter woman.

However, when he said, "I understand. It hurts me that it's over too, but we can at least still be a family for our kids' sake," I was devastated that he was not willing to fight for me. That meant that he also felt like there was no hope. I stood there in a daze, wondering had the last eight years been a fantasy or some dream that I made up in my mind. There had been some bad, but there had been a lot of good that obviously meant nothing.

The realization left me speechless as he walked up to me, wrapped his arm softly around my waist, kissed my forehead and said again, "I'm sorry, Jada. I really am."

Then he walked out of the kitchen. Tears started to sting my eyes as they formed. To my surprise, they weren't sad tears. They were tears that appreciated my reality. It was a hard pill to swallow that me and Dolla were officially over, but it was something that needed to happened. I could no longer be this woman who was so ride or die until I killed myself with the stupid decisions that I was making to continuously forgive. I had to be as loyal to myself as I was to him, which meant knowing that I deserved a man that was as loyal to me as I was to him.

KENNEDY

Once leaving the clinic, I was able to make it to Meech's house in time for Elijah's party. I was shocked to see King in the driveway as I pulled up, and he was surprised to see me as well. I was surprised to be there myself, but after leaving the clinic, I felt like I had to be. Plus, Jada knew that Dolla would be there, and she needed me there for moral support, so said the many text messages she'd sent me as I was leaving the clinic.

Me and King weakly spoke to each other as we entered the house. It was obvious that, besides surprised, he was also relieved to see that I was there. I knew that since I was there for Jada, he would still include me in this moment that he was about to have with Elijah, but that it was something I chose to deal with on my way there. Again, I was sacrificing for my people, but Jada was someone that I knew I could make sacrifices for. If anybody had been ride or die with no question, it was Jada.

"You sure you okay with being here?" King asked me.

As we walked through the front door, I didn't want to burst his bubble by telling him that I was there by default. So, I simply shrugged and said, "I'm just here."

My mind was full of so many thoughts. I didn't know if I was coming or going, or if the decisions I had made earlier that day were right or wrong. I was in the daze as Meech walked towards me and King as we stood in the foyer.

Meech looked both surprised and happy to see me as well, as he spoke to us, "What's up, y'all?"

We both greeted him, and then King immediately asked, "Where is he?"

King had obviously been very eager to have this moment with Elijah, but getting rid of Siren was a priority that had kept him from doing so. Now, King was more than ready to be the father that he hadn't been able to be to Elijah for so many years. That made me realize the man that King really was, outside of that one moment of disloyalty. *This* was the man that I fell in love with, that I went to jail for. He had an undying love for his family, blood or not. That made me want to risk anything for him all over again.

Meech said, "He's in the back in the pool. Let me go get him. We'll meet you in the den."

Meech went towards the back of the house as King and I went to the den. As we sat on the couch, I saw the nervousness in King's eyes. I had to put my feelings aside to be there for him. I put my arm around his shoulder and started to rub it soothingly, telling him, "It's going to be okay. You can do this."

"I just feel bad for shorty. I know Meech has been a great father to him, but I also know that he's wanted to know his real dad. I don't want him to hate me, thinking that I've been around him for all these years and didn't want to be a father to him or some shit."

"He might not get it now because he's so young, but he will eventually understand. He's always looked up to you and loved you. He'll be excited to know that Uncle King is actually his dad."

King took a deep breath. It seemed as if he was trying to believe everything that I had just said. He was about to say something when Elijah ran into the den. He was wrapped in a towel but was still dripping wet. His swimming trunks were dripping water all over the carpet.

Me and King laughed at the way his eyeballs were full of excitement as he told King, "Hey, Uncle King! It's my birthday!"

Even Meech chuckled as he sat on the couch beside King.

When King smiled at Elijah, it was a different smile than he had given him before. It was admiration and more loving. King was looking at Elijah as if Elijah was his future, his son, and it was so touching.

"I know, man," he told Elijah. "I got you a present too."

"For real? Give it to me!" Elijah said as he stuck his hand out.

We all laughed as King told him, "I will when you open your presents. But I have to tell you something first."

Elijah asked him, "What? Is it about my mom? Daddy already told me. She had to go away for a while. She isn't feeling well."

"I know, man," King told him. "But I have to tell you something else." Then he took a deep breath and hesitated. It seemed as if we were all holding our breath as King figured out the right words to say. "Meech is your dad. He's been raising you since he and your mom were boyfriend and girlfriend. You know that, right?" Elijah nodded his head, and King continued. "And Meech is always going to be your dad..." When King's voice cracked, I instantly felt my own tears coming. King forced out the rest of the words that he had to say. "Well, I...I know you've been looking for your father, the man that made you, and I just found out that I'm that man. I'm your father."

Elijah's eyes bucked, and it made my tears fall as I watched his little mind attempt to make sense of everything that King had just said.

He asked slowly and hesitantly, "Yooou're my daddy?"

King nodded and told him, "Yea."

Elijah's head cocked dramatically to the side as he asked, "For real?"

And then, when his smile seemed to be forcing its way through his confused expression, we all were relieved and started to smile as well.

King immediately reached out for Elijah and hugged him, despite the fact that he was soaking wet and getting King's Gucci shirt soaking wet. "Yeah, man, for real," he told Elijah. "I'm your father."

Elijah hugged him so tightly that I was no longer able to hold back my tears. Then I looked over at Meech, who was allowing his tears to flow, and I completely broke down! I was like a fucking baby as I sat there on that couch watching King and Elijah embrace as if they were just meeting each other for the first time. They *were* actually meeting each other for the first time. They had already known each other, but they were now officially meeting each other as father and son.

Then I saw Elijah's eyes buck. He took his arms from around King and told him, "You have a daughter!" He looked at me and then asked King, "I have a sister then, right?"

"Yep," I answered for King. "...And you might have *another* sister or a brother."

Not only did Elijah's eyes buck, but so did King's after his head whipped around towards me. I had to giggle. Both of their responses were so funny. Just looking in their eyes made me feel better about changing my mind as I laid on that table in the examination room. Just as the anesthesiologist was putting the needle in my arm, something told me that I was making a big mistake. No matter the mistakes that King had made, I always wanted to be just as loyal to him as I had always been. I was not going to change who I was because of the hurt that was in my heart. I knew that he wanted this baby, and I also wanted nothing more than to have the family that I always had, and I refused to give Siren the satisfaction of knowing that she had torn my family apart.

I hadn't seen that much happiness in King's eyes in a long time as he asked me, "You pregnant?"

I grinned as I answered, "Yep."

He threw his arms around me and hugged me so tightly as he told me, "Man, this is the happiest day of my life... But it'll make it so much better if you tell me that I can come back home."

I put my hands on his chest and pushed back so that I could look into his eyes. Then I kissed his lips softly.

Feeling the same love that I had always felt when I was with my King, I knew that no matter what, my sacrifices were not in vain. He was still my King, I was still his queen, and my world wouldn't be right if I wasn't sitting on the throne next to *my* nigga. "Yes, baby, you can come home."

EPILOGUE

Two months later, the crew was once again at a celebration. This time, the celebration was held at Pearl's. The restaurant was filled with members of the crew, close friends, and family.

"My nigga!" Meech approached his cousin, Brooklyn, with a huge grin on his face and his arms outstretched to hug Brooklyn. London was of course by Meech's side. She wouldn't have missed Brooklyn's homecoming for the world. Plus, she would always be next to her man. She and Meech were officially a couple, and things had been going better than expected.

"What up, Cuz? It's good to be home," Brooklyn said as he embraced Meech.

It was indeed good to be home, but Brooklyn never doubted that the crew would come through for him. He wasn't surprised when, during his court appearance the day before, the judge had dismissed his case because of an unavailable witness, who was necessary to prove that the defendant committed the crime and loss of evidence necessary to prove that the defendant committed the crime. In layman's terms, unexpectedly the evidence against Brooklyn had disappeared and so had Detective Jefferies.

"Broooooklyn!" Suddenly, Kennedy's squeaky voice filled the air. Though not that far along, she already had the pregnancy glow. Her smile was so bright as she held King's hand with her right hand and Elijah's with her left. As she and King embraced and spoke to Brooklyn, Meech embraced with his son. Though King was Elijah's biological father, he and Meech had come to an agreement to share custody of Elijah so that the bond between Meech and Elijah would never be broken. The moment that Elijah learned who his father was, the tension between King and Meech vanished. Without further discussion, Meech had forgiven King, and King vowed to show him and Kennedy for the rest of his life that he deserved that forgiveness.

"About time they let this big nigga out of jail." Once hearing Dolla's voice, everyone turned around to see him and Jada coming through the crowd towards them. Kennedy let out a sigh of relief as she watched Jada walk next to Dolla. Kennedy was so relieved that Jada and Dolla were finally getting along. Their relationship was still very much over. Dolla was focusing on being a good father to his four kids, and Jada was focused on establishing herself. She was helping Kennedy manage the boutique, Queen Carter, as well as focusing on the launch of her own hair company, Simply Pretty Hair, of which Dolla had financed.

Meanwhile, at Logan's Correctional Women's Prison, Siren had always found it a wicked coincidence that she had wound up in the same prison that Kennedy had served her time. But on this particular night, as she stood trapped in a corner of the dark, musty, bathroom staring into the murderous eyes of two of her fellow inmates, she looked at the shanks in their hands and found this grossly coincidental.

Of course I would die this way. Shit.

"Gustavo sent you?" she asked through heavy breaths, in assumption since the women were Spanish.

The tallest woman with long, auburn hair smiled devilishly. "No. We were sent by *King*."

Siren's heart dropped violently to her feet. She never expected this. She had done as King told her to; she had taken the plea deal and was doing her time. But she was foolish to think that King would allow her to get away with setting up his precious Kennedy and hiding his esteemed prince from him. Siren had done the unthinkable, the unforgivable, and the ultimate revenge was owed to everyone who had suffered from her lies and deception. After she had taken the deal, King watched his family and his crew and realized that her punishment just wasn't savage enough for what she had attempted to destroy. Opps had done less to the crew, yet had suffered way worse. It was only fair that Siren suffered the same.

"You ready to die, bitch?" the short one with a pageboy haircut sneered.

Though Siren was shivering from the fear of death on the inside, she remained a true bitch on the outside. She kept silent but stood her ground with a sneer as the two Spanish women charged her, first slicing her neck and then stabbing viscously into her heart until her curdling screams stopped, her eyes slowly closed, and her breathing ceased. To be sure that she was dead, the inmate with the long hair checked Siren's pulse.

"She's dead, Christina," she said to the other. "Let him know."

Christina reached under the sink, removed some tile, put her arm into the wall and retrieved a cell phone. She took a picture of Siren's lifeless body, then quickly sent a text message and returned the phone to its hiding place.

Back at Pearl's, King felt his phone vibrate so allowed one of his hands to leave Kennedy's waist. They continued to slow dance as he quickly opened the message and returned the phone to his pocket with a smile.

"It's done?" Kennedy asked with eager eyes.

King returned his arm to her waist, saying, "Yea, it's done, baby."

Kennedy exhaled and then rested her head on King's shoulder, feeling vindicated. It was only right that Siren's blood was spilling on the same floor that Kennedy's tears had shed for three years.

No matter what the crew had gone through, no matter the changes, and even though some members were gone and some were new, the Carter dynasty was now stronger than ever. The last few months of deceit and trouble had only strengthened their bond and proven to everyone that they were not to be broken.

Now, they were *truly* going to live happily ever after.

The End!

Jessica N. Watkins was born April 1st in Chicago, Illinois. She obtained a Bachelors of Arts with Focus in Psychology from DePaul University and Masters of Applied Professional Studies with focus in Business Administration from the like institution. Working in Hospital Administration for the majority of her career, Watkins has also been an author of fiction literature since the young age of nine. Eventually she used writing as an outlet during her freshmen year of high school as a single parent: "In the third grade I entered a short story contest with a fiction tale of an apple tree that refused to grow despite the efforts of the darling main character. My writing evolved from apple trees to my seventh and eighth grade classmates paying me to read novels I wrote about kids our age living the lives our parents wouldn't dare let us". At the age of thirty-three, Watkins' chronicles have matured into steamy, humorous, and realistic tales of African American Romance and Urban Fiction.

In September 2013, Jessica's most recent novel, Secrets of a Side Bitch, published by SBR Publications, reached #1 on multiple charts.

Jessica N. Watkins is available for talks, workshops or book signings. Email her for more information at jessica@femistrypress.net

Follow Jessica:
Instagram: @authorjwatkins
Twitter: @authorjwatkins
Facebook: @jwpresents
Facebook Group:
https://www.facebook.com/groups/femistryfans

CPSIA information can be obtained
at www.ICGtesting.com
Printed in the USA
LVHW051741131218
600170LV00017B/342/P